SOD HOUSE ADVENTURE

by

BONNIE BESS WORLINE

Illustrated by Kathleen Voute

LONGMANS, GREEN AND CO.

New York · London · Toronto · 1956

LONGMANS, GREEN AND CO., INC.
55 FIFTH AVENUE, NEW YORK 3

LONGMANS, GREEN AND CO., Ltd.
6 & 7 CLIFFORD STREET, LONDON W 1

LONGMANS, GREEN AND CO.
20 CRANFIELD ROAD, TORONTO 16

SOD HOUSE ADVENTURE

FIRST EDITION

LIBRARY OF CONGRESS CATALOG CARD NUMBER 56-7870

Printed in the United States of America

To

RICHARD *and* VIOLA

MARION *and* HARRIET

who helped to make Kansas

and to

APRIL MARIAN *and* COURTNER

who wanted to know about them

ILLUSTRATIONS

SOD HOUSE
ADVENTURE

CHAPTER 1

HARTLEY AND PHOEBE DAWSON HAD BEEN SENT BY THEIR mother to fix the tail vane of the windmill. In the great expanse of pancake-level prairie where they lived, the high tower of the windmill was the only real landmark. Surrounded by miles of stretching bluestem grass and sunflowers of the summer, their little house made of sod seemed to have grown in its place like a special kind of prairie plant. Now, under a coating of heavy spring snow, the fields and house and stable were just a broad white background for the dark outline of the square wooden tower topped by its twelve-foot wheel. Mother said the windmill was an exclamation mark on empty-seeming land; it said to any traveler, "People live here!"

But like everything else on the prairie claim, the windmill was for use, not decoration. The tower had been built high and strong to support the big wheel, and the wheel, made of a series of carefully placed wide spokes, was turned by the fierce, almost never-ending winds of the plains. By an arrangement of gears, the turning wheel lifted and dropped, lifted and dropped a bar that extended down the center of the tower to ground level. There the bar was bolted to a pump which in turn reached down more than a hundred feet into the ground.

Each turn of the wheel in the high wind pumped up water into a metal tank some fifteen feet across. This was the water for all the Dawson family, and for their cows, chickens, pigs, sheep, and pony. There was no other water closer than the West Branch, a shallow creek about four miles west. There was no other well within ten or twelve miles.

Unless the children could get the windmill to pump again, they would be out of water until their father got home, except for what they might be able to pump by hand after unbolting the long bar. But even their father would have had hard work pumping as much water as was needed, and he had been gone almost four weeks now. He had left with a wagon train to bring back supplies, and they had no way of knowing when he would be back.

"I think it came loose where Dad wired it before," Hartley said, leaning back to look at the machinery high above them. "I held it for him, I know what to do. We'll both have to go up; you hold it and I'll wire it."

"Mother said to be sure to turn off the wheel before you go up," Phoebe reminded him. She thought it looked a long way to the top, but not for anything would she have had Hartley, who was younger than she, dream she was not as delighted over a chance to climb the windmill as he was. Usually that was a forbidden thrill.

Hartley said indignantly, "Aw, who needs to be told that? I guess no one has to tell me to turn off the windmill before I climb it."

He braced himself against the wind, and turned the crank that wound a chain to stop the wheel. Then he scurried up the narrow ladder to the top with swift sureness. Phoebe, wearing a pair of her father's old overalls, followed him more cautiously.

The tail vane was indeed loose. It was a huge, thin, flat projection fastened to the wheel, and was designed to catch the wind, however it might shift direction, and to change the angle of the creaking wheel so that always it would receive the full power of the breeze. Now, with the connecting rod broken, the wheel only occasionally spun around and then drifted out of position and stopped. Hartley quickly made an emergency splice which he thought would hold until his father returned. Then the children lingered on the high platform, scanning the far-stretching horizons, north, south, east and west.

The windmill was some twenty feet high, the prairie as level as a floor, so from the platform they could see for miles in every direction. Off to the west there was a narrow strip of gray, where trees bordered the small creek that ran near the edge of their claim. The rest of the ground was a glaring white, as the snow from the recent late storm reflected the hard, bright afternoon sun. No buildings broke the even surface, except for their own small sod house below, and the longer sod barn beyond the corral. The Martins, their nearest neighbors, were to the west beyond the horizon line, and the neighbors in the other directions were even farther away.

Phoebe and Hartley knew they would see no buildings, but sometimes they could see jack rabbits hopping across the prairie, or hawks swooping through the sky. Sometimes even in the winter, on warm, windless days, little prairie dogs would venture out of their snug homes underground. But today Phoebe and Hartley watched hopefully for horses and wagons to appear from the northeast. Even with the unexpected return of snow with the late spring storm, it was well past the time their father had expected to get back. They looked in vain, however. The horizon to the northeast was as empty as usual, and they were about to climb back down the ladder when something on the south edge of the prairie caught Hartley's eye.

"Phoebe, look — right there." He pointed. "Do you see something moving?"

"Where?" Phoebe asked, and then, following the line of his outstretched hand, she saw it, too.

A small dark shadow moved steadily along the edge of snow and sky, and as it grew larger they knew that it was coming toward them. Breathlessly they watched. It grew bigger and bigger, until at last they could make out for certain the outline of a horse and rider. The horse was making good time.

"What can it be?" Phoebe wondered.

"We'd better tell Mother," Hartley said, and he began running backward down the windmill ladder. Phoebe followed almost as quickly, and they raced to the sod house.

"Mother!" Hartley shouted as he burst through the door. "Someone's coming — about three miles away, south."

Phoebe, right behind him, added, "He's coming fast, at a steady lope."

Mrs. Dawson jumped up in alarm, moving instinctively toward the rifle hanging over the fireplace. "One — alone?" she asked.

"Just one. We watched to see. We were just finishing the windmill, and looking for any signs of Father's wagons. We looked around, and there he was."

Mrs. Dawson said thoughtfully, "One man riding alone probably is bringing news. Some of the settlers to the south beyond the river were going with the train — they may have had word. Pray that it is good."

As she spoke she threw some corn cobs onto the fire. When it blazed up, she added a stick of hedge wood and moved the teakettle over to heat faster. "I do hope the men have been sighted," she said. "It seems like four years since your father left."

The littlest sister, Mary Ann, whimpered weakly in the cradle, and Phoebe gently rocked it.

"It's because the children have been sick that the time has seemed so long. If Father had had any idea they were getting croup, I think he never would have gone," she said.

"We could have waited for the boards for our house, but salt and meal and the other supplies we had to have. I am glad Father has not had the worry of knowing they were sick, for now all four are much better. Hartley, the rider must be nearly here — go out to stable his horse. I think I will use a little of the coffee, for your father will surely be here soon with the new supply, and a rider in this weather will be cold through and through. Phoebe, bring some of the corn bread, and some sorghum and cottage cheese. David, don't hang on Mother's skirts so — you'll be stepped on, sure. Sit with Tessie and Martha and Robbie there by the fire."

Steps on the crunchy, packed snow told them the traveler had come. Phoebe ran to open the door. A slim figure in breeches and heavy jacket, and a cap almost covered by a wide wool scarf, stepped in. Mrs. Dawson watched the stranger closely, but she said courteously:

"This is wild weather for traveling, sir. Come to the fire."

The rider stamped his feet a little, as though to start the circulation, and pulled off the heavy scarf and cap. It was a girl! She was not quite grown up, although older than Phoebe by several years.

"You are Mrs. Dawson?" the girl asked eagerly. "Oh, ma'am, I'm so glad to find you. I am Marietta Stephens. My folks have the claim on the far side of the river. We came last year from the east."

"Why, come get warm, child. I heard my husband speak of your folks. Your father went with the wagon train, I believe?"

"Yes, and my mother is sick. She's been sick quite a while. I kept thinking Papa would get home, and I did all I knew, but she is worse, much worse. We are going to

Phoebe opened the door

have a new baby, but she thought Papa would be home before it came. She said if he didn't come she would tell me just what to do. Now she is too sick to make sense when she talks to us. She seems to think she's back home in Virginia and keeps talking to my grandmother who lives there. She throws off the cover and says she is too hot, although the house is not warm. Then she calls for Papa, and calls him, and she doesn't seem to know me at all. Oh, please, ma'am, tell me what to do. I must hurry back, for I left my brothers and sister to care for the little ones and Mother; the oldest is only ten, and they are very frightened."

The girl had tears in her eyes and in her voice, but she did not cry.

While the girl was talking, Mrs. Dawson began taking off the heavy wraps, and pulled her to the seat by the fire. She said to Phoebe, "Pull off her shoes and rub her feet." She herself set the warmed bread and hot coffee before Marietta. "Eat and drink. You must get warm and rested."

At that moment Hartley dashed in to say he had rubbed the horse, and fed and watered and blanketed him. Hartley was curious about the stranger. He had seen her only briefly as he had taken the horse and directed the stranger to the house. Now he stopped in his tracks, amazed to find a girl.

"Je-hos-a-phat!" he exclaimed, as he had heard his father do. His mother did not take time to scold him.

"Hartley, hitch Captain to the sleigh. Check every bit

of harness. I want no breaks on the way, and if we hit some slushy places there may be hard pulling. I must go to Mrs. Stephens. Phoebe, you will be in charge here, but you mustn't be bossy. Remember, Hartley is almost as old as you are. If you plan together and don't quarrel, you will manage all right. You're not afraid?"

The last was a statement, rather than a question. Phoebe answered a little uncertainly, "No — no, I'm not afraid, Mother, except — the little ones. They've been so sick."

Mrs. Dawson looked tenderly at the four little figures snuggled together on the fireplace bench, too awed by the stranger to make a sound, and watching their mother with big eyes.

"I know, dear," she said. "But they are better now, and our neighbor must have help. You know how to keep them warm, and how to feed them. All that is needed is to be dependable, and I'm sure you will be. Hartley, you must do the milking, and feed and water the stock. Get in the water and fuel, for Sister will be too busy to help. Now run get the sleigh ready. Oh, yes, if I'm gone more than one day, and your father does not come, be sure to break the ice in the tank morning and night, so it won't get too thick. You can help with the little ones, too. Tell them stories and play with them so they won't fret. Well, go now . . ."

Shy Tessie, who was the oldest of what Hartley and Phoebe called "the children," put her hand into her mother's.

"I can help, too," she said. "I'm getting very big."

Her mother bent and kissed her. "Of course you can,

dear. You can rock the baby's cradle, and play house with Martha, and not quarrel with the boys. David and Robbie, you must not fight, and not fuss about bedtime. All of you mind Phoebe, and help her take good care of you until Mother gets back."

She turned to Marietta, who had been watching and listening with feelings too strong for speech.

"We will both go back in our sleigh, and you can leave your horse here." As she spoke she began moving quietly around the room, gathering wraps and bundling up.

Marietta said, "I don't know how to thank you, ma'am. My mother wouldn't ask you to leave your own children alone. If you would just tell me what to do — it's very kind of you to offer to come, but my mother would not want to impose on anyone."

Mrs. Dawson went right on with her preparations.

"It is no imposition, Marietta. Settlers here, where we are all so far apart, must stand by each other, or we would all be lost. If you are warm now, you had best get your things on again. I'm almost ready, and we haven't much time before dark."

Very soon Hartley had the light sleigh and pony at the door. Warmed buffalo robes were laid in, Mrs. Dawson and Marietta seated themselves close together on the single seat. Then hot stones that Phoebe had laid in the fire were wrapped and put at their feet, the big robes were pulled up around them, and they were ready to start.

Mrs. Dawson had kissed the younger children good-by in the house. She knelt, with them all huddling as close to her as they could get, while she asked their Heavenly Father to care for them while she was gone, to protect the absent fathers and to bring health to their sick neighbor. Together they prayed, "God be with us, while we are absent, one from another." Now, although they could not see much through the oiled paper on the windows, she waved and called "Good-by." Phoebe and Hartley, having helped tuck in the robes, watched their mother loosen the reins and shake them to signal Captain to start.

"Good-by! Good-by!" the brother and sister shouted, and they waved until the sleigh began to grow smaller in the distance.

"Come on, Phoebe," Hartley suggested, "we can watch them a long while yet from the windmill."

"Oh, let's," cried Phoebe eagerly. Then she heard a whimper from within the thick walls of the house. The children were crying, and they were alone! They were in her charge now. She must take care of them.

"I can't, Hart," she called after him. "The children are crying, and one might fall in the fire. I'll go to them. You go ahead and watch."

She lingered one last minute to see the moving sleigh grow smaller and smaller toward the horizon. She fought the empty, sinking feeling inside of her. The wide, stretching prairie was suddenly very lonely, with no one, nothing, as far as she could look in any direction except for that one dear, moving spot that threatened any moment to lose itself in space. Phoebe began to feel very young and helpless and alone, and she wanted to cry. But as she wiped her eyes and stepped back inside the soddy, four little people flung themselves upon her. They were all crying, yet they clung to her.

David said, "It's all right for Mamma to go away. Sister is here, and she's a big girl."

Phoebe brushed her eyes and squatted down to hug all of them at once. She knew now, for sure, that whatever came, she would be a big girl, just as Mother and Father expected her to be.

CHAPTER 2

Phoebe cuddled each of the little brothers and sisters until they quit crying, but she knew that they would easily start again as they thought of their mother being gone. Bedtimes, she could foresee, would be a trial for them all.

"I must keep them busy," she thought. "What can I do?" Just then the baby began to cry in the big hooded cradle, and Phoebe said to the others, "Just listen! Mary Ann is waking up, and she has had such a good nap. Let's see if she wants her clothes changed."

"Let me, Phoebe. Oh, do let me," begged Tessie. "I'm sure I could, and you know Mother said I was to help take care of her."

Phoebe thought a minute. "I don't see why not. I'll help you."

"No, I want to do it all by myself," protested Tessie. "I'll hold my finger in front of the pin, and not let it stick her a bit."

"Well, all right."

"Me, too, I want to, too," immediately chimed in David

14

and Robbie. Even small Martha, who had only just moved out of the cradle when Mary Ann came, chirped, "Me, too."

"No, just Tessie until Mama comes home. You know, Mary Ann has been sick, and we must not disturb her too much. No, David, Sister said no. But you may hold her in your lap in the big chair, like Mama lets you. And so may Robbie. And then Martha can rock the cradle to help her go to sleep. All right? See, Martha, pretty soon you can rock the cradle for Mary Ann."

When, after one or two trials, Tessie got Mary Ann's dry clothes pinned smoothly, and had carefully tied the strings on the long wool knit bootees so her feet would stay covered and warm, David climbed into the Big Chair their father had made. It had a wooden framework and was lined with sheepskin from one of their own sheep, and made a wonderfully cozy place. Phoebe lifted the baby, pulled her long petticoats and dress down smoothly, and laid her, a snug little bundle, between David's knees. He lovingly clasped his arms around her middle and sat very still while she leaned against him and the others gathered around. Mary Ann looked up at her brothers and smiled and began to talk. She did not say anything, but she talked and talked, and Martha and Robbie laughed and clapped their hands.

Then it was Robbie's turn to hold Mary Ann. Hartley came in, having watched from the top of the windmill until his mother's sleigh had disappeared into the great stretching whiteness, and now he was glad to be close to the others, like a puppy coming back to the litter. He did not want to remember how alone they were. He noticed little Martha's drooping lips and the tears in her big blue eyes.

"Martha hold a ba-by," she pleaded.

Hartley laughed. He picked her up and seated her on his shoulders, which usually made her squeal with delight. But not this time.

"Martha hold Hartley. How will that be?" he suggested, and he swung her down onto the big bed built onto the side of the wall, then pretended to sit on her lap. He carefully braced his feet on the floor and sat very gently on her.

Now, indeed, she crowed and laughed. She reached her arms as far as she could around him, and called, "See! Martha hold a big baby."

Phoebe left Hartley with the children while she went to the unheated storeroom adjoining their one-room home. It was dug into the ground, and was built up very little above the ground level. Because of this, and the fact that no wind could get through the solid earth walls, the temperature did not go below freezing in it, and food stored there kept very well.

Father had made bins to hold potatoes and onions off the damp floor, and cabbages and beets were packed in boxes of sand. A half barrel in the corner held sauerkraut, and several stone jars were filled with pickles and salt pork. On hooks overhead were sacks of dried corn and dried apples and peaches. There, also, hung the smoked pork and the dried jerked beef. Another barrel held molasses made from the sorghum cane on their own place, and on one shelf was a large jar of wild honey Father had taken from the bees. All the pleasant food smells mingled with the moist, special smell of the earth walls and floor.

Phoebe stood a moment enjoying the snug feeling of having so much food on hand. She could remember earlier years when Father had not been used to the climate, and they were just getting started. The crops then had not been good, and Phoebe had shared her mother's anxiety about the small stores of food which dwindled and dwindled, yet must last until the next crop was ready at the end of the summer.

Now there was plenty, and Father would bring back not only salt and fine-ground corn meal, but also some flour and a little white sugar, for treats. There would also be cloth for their clothes for the next year, and new tools, and all the little needs that must be supplied from the far-off trading center. But this time, best of all, he was actually bringing boards for the new frame house he and mother had planned so long.

It would be a two-story house with two rooms downstairs one for cooking and eating. Above there would be the same space divided by partitions for separate sleeping rooms for Mother and Father, the girls, and the boys. The house was to have an iron stove instead of just a fireplace, and windows with real glass.

They had talked over every detail of it for months, and

it would be very elegant, Phoebe supposed. But she wondered if it would ever seem as homey as the dear, whitewashed soddy with all of them tumbling over each other.

Now she looked around at the supplies, wondering what to have for supper. It made her feel quite grown-up to be deciding all by herself, without consulting Mother. Thoughtfully she took the cover off the sauerkraut barrel and gouged out a good hunk of the cool, tangy stuff in her fingers to eat, just as a bit of celebration of not having any grownup around to catch her. She decided on potato and cabbage soup with some dried beef boiled in it, and cold corn bread with butter and peach butter.

Tomorrow, she thought, I must set the oven over the fire and bake more corn bread so we don't run out, and if Mother is gone two days, it will be time to churn. I shall do it all by myself, and mold the butter just beautifully.

How glad she was that she knew how, although she could remember more than once having rebelled at being obliged to lift that old dasher, again and again and again, when she wanted to play outdoors.

She took some of the soft mush which Mother had already cooked for hours until it was creamy, and then stored so that it only needed to be warmed for the baby. Phoebe dipped it in a pan, then carefully covered the mush again, and added milk from the crock of the morning milking to her pan. She paused on her way out to put half a dozen apples from the apple barrel into her skirt. While Mary Ann's supper warmed, she let the apples roast in the front of the fire, in the ashes.

Hartley saw what she was doing and asked, "Can I feed her, Phoebe?"

"You're supposed to milk."

"I know, but I've got plenty of time. It's still very light."

"And feed the chickens and water everything, and get the eggs."

"I know, I know — I guess I know better than you do what all there is to do in the barn. And I know how long it will take."

"All right, if you're sure."

Phoebe tied a bib around Mary Ann's neck. Hartley held the baby carefully in his left arm and spooned very thin mush into her rosebud mouth.

"She's eating good — see, Phoebe. She's eating better than she has since she was sick. She just wanted her brother to feed her, didn't you, old girl?"

"Phoebe," Martha began to beg, "Martha eat, too. Hartley feed Martha mush?"

But there was so little fine meal left, until Father came, that Phoebe was afraid to spare it. There was so little that Mary Ann could eat.

"I'll tell you, Martha, you can have an apple with Tessie and the boys. You can eat an apple just like Hartley does, when he finishes feeding baby. You're a big girl now. Just the baby eats mush."

"I'm a big girl?"

"Of course you are. Now, here, you can all eat your apples. They're warm, anyway. And Sister will get supper."

Martha sat beside Tessie, and Phoebe gave them each a

spoon and an apple. Tessie dug hers out and ate it with
her spoon, but the boys, after a bite or so, gave up and
ate theirs like raw apples, which they almost were. Tessie
helped Martha spoon hers out, but Martha soon imitated
the boys. They all sat on their little bench and chewed
solemnly, while Mary Ann smacked her lips over her mush,
and Phoebe made another trip to the storeroom.

She brought back potatoes and cabbage and the dried
beef, cut them all into small pieces, and set them merrily
simmering in the big iron pot over the fire.

When Mary Ann began to bubble mush, Phoebe took
her while Hartley downed his apple in four bites to the
admiration of his little brothers. Then he bundled up
again in his jacket and overshoes to do the chores in the
barn.

For a few minutes Phoebe held the baby up against her
shoulder. She enjoyed Mary Ann's sweet, cuddly feel in her
arms, and hated to put her down. But there were still many
things to do, and Phoebe must not sit still long. She told
Tessie to smooth the pillow and blankets in the cradle, then
she tucked the drowsy baby into her nest.

"Now she's just like a little bird, and Martha, you can
rock her. Tessie, you help. Not too hard — you'll spill her
out. And we will all sh-h-h so she can sleep."

But Martha pushed Tessie's hand away from the cradle
hood.

"No, Tessie! Just Martha!" she insisted.

Phoebe whispered to Tessie, "Just stand by so she doesn't

Phoebe laid the cloth on the table

push too hard. Pretty soon she will be tired and quit, and then you can do it."

She winked at Tessie, and Tessie felt grown-up to be in Phoebe's secret, and so much bigger than Martha. Patiently she waited, and sure enough, very soon Martha noticed that the boys were playing in their corner by the fireplace with some string and corncobs, making a play fence. When Martha drifted over to squat down and watch them, Tessie quietly took over the baby. It was her baby, now, and she was pretending she was the oldest, and Mama had gone away and left her in charge. Long after Mary Ann, her thumb comfortable in her mouth, was sleeping peacefully, Tessie rocked the cradle back and forth. Phoebe started to ask her to set the table. Then she saw Tessie's faraway, dreamy expression and said nothing; instead she did it herself.

"She's having a lovely make-believe; I won't disturb her," Phoebe said to herself, as she laid the red-and-white checkered cloth on the rough boards of the homemade table, and set out the thick plates and mugs and tin spoons, with a knife at her own plate to spread bread for all of them.

In time Hartley brought in the pail of evening milk and seven eggs.

"Everything is as snug as if Father was here, Phoebe," he announced. "I fed and watered everything, that girl's horse, too, and the chickens and all. There's cobs and wood ready and the water barrel is full and no ice in the windmill pond. Um! Cabbage! Smells good."

He dipped water into the washbasin on its low bench, made a great lather with the bar of homemade soap, and delighted the younger ones by blowing big bubbles through his clenched fists.

"Now don't dawdle. I'm just ready to take up supper," Phoebe scolded gently very much in Mother's tones.

"Oh, keep your pants on," Hartley retorted. But he rinsed his hands, washed the boys, and soon they were all seated around the table. Martha's high stool was near Phoebe, and Hartley sat at Father's place at the end. Although there were six of them, the table seemed empty.

Phoebe said to Hartley, "You ask the blessing, as Father does; you are in his place."

Hartley was pleased, and also very solemn as he remembered again how far away their parents were. All of them were thankful to feel that God, at least, was still there.

Phoebe strained the warm milk, ladled out soup, and spread butter and peach butter on corn bread for everyone before she tasted her own food. There were disadvantages, she realized, in being the mother.

She felt it even more when the meal was over, and Hartley began to help with the corncob play, while she must do the dishes. If Mother had been home Phoebe would have complained that Hartley should help. But she had no good excuse. He had done his chores without help from her. So she resolutely stacked the plates. She brought the pan for dishwater and the pan for rinsing, poured in hot water from the teakettle and cooled it with several dipperfuls from the water barrel. Then she began rubbing the soap bar in the dishcloth energetically to get a good lather.

"Phoebe, I'll help with the dishes," Tessie offered.

"Why, Tessie, that's a dear. But you needn't, Mother didn't say to, you know. You go play."

"But I want to. And tomorrow I will peel the potatoes, because pretty soon I'll be a big girl too, and I must get used to it."

Phoebe looked at the earnest face, with its serious, big brown eyes so intent upon her. She stooped quickly and kissed her.

"That's right, dear, you are really growing up, aren't you? I'll be glad of your help. I really am a little tired."

"It's fun working together, " Tessie said, as she happily got out a dish towel. And then Martha must have one, too. So Phoebe stood her up on a chair, and Tessie sorted out the spoons for her to wipe. She gleefully polished each one and then started over again, while the two older girls made quick work of the rest.

Soon the dishes were all neatly put away in the cupboard, the left-over food covered and carried to the storeroom, and the hard-packed clay floor swept neat with the corn broom they had helped Father make. Phoebe rinsed the towels out in the dishwater, emptied the water into the slop pail, wiped both pans carefully, inside and out, and hung them, one over the other, on their nail at the side of the cupboard. She did not slight any part of the job, for this time no one but herself could check to be sure it was done thoroughly.

The oiled paper in the windows let in little light at best. Now the room was growing dusky and the light from the fire made queer shadows seem to dance around the room. When Mother and Father were home, the whole family liked to play with the shadows. By standing in front of the fire, and moving fingers and hands and legs, or two standing close together, they could make funny pictures on the whitewashed wall opposite. Each in turn would try, and sometimes they would all laugh until they could not sit still. But now, with Mother and Father so far away, the shadows did not seem funny. They were weird and scary.

David said suddenly, "There's a boogey man under the table."

"Hush, David," Phoebe told him, trying to quiet her own fears. "There is no such thing as a boogey man. You know Father said so."

For answer David began to cry, "I want Father! I'm afraid!"

Robbie and Martha immediately took it up, and Hartley told them crossly to be still, which did not help. Phoebe said softly to herself, "Oh, dear, whatever am I going to do now."

Martha tried to crawl into Phoebe's lap, and Phoebe felt that in one more moment she would be crying harder than any of them.

A soft hand squeezed into hers. Tessie asked in a trembling voice, "Are you afraid, Phoebe?"

Just then, above the noise of the children came the penetrating, mournful howl of a coyote.

"No, I'm not afraid," snapped Phoebe loudly. She spoke crossly because she really was afraid. She was trying to convince herself.

"Then," said Tessie confidently, "I'm not going to be

afraid, either, because I'm a big girl, too." She let go of
Phoebe, walked over to the corner by the fireplace where
the children had their playthings, and began deliberately
and noisily to change the fence, with a sly glance at the
crying boys.

David took his fists out of his eyes to see what was
going on, and at once forgot to cry. He ran toward Tessie,
shouting, "Don't you touch that! That's ours! That's not
for girls, is it, Robbie?"

"No!" agreed Robbie, likewise forgetting to cry. "It's
mine!"

"It is not, it's both of ours, but you can't have it, Tessie."

"Oh, all right. I didn't want it, anyway. I just came
to get Araminta," Tessie said, calmly putting down the
fence and picking up her corn doll.

"Well, did you see that!" Phoebe exclaimed quietly to
Hartley, who grinned and nodded.

The boys, their minds again on their play, sat down
to repair what they considered the damage. Hartley helped
them by suggesting they play that Indians had cut their
fence to raid the cattle and been caught just in time.
Phoebe sat down with Martha to sing her a lullaby, and
Tessie sat beside her with Araminta.

Araminta had begun as an ear of corn. On a piece of cloth
Mother had painted a face, using bluing for the eyes and
iron rust for the hair. She had stitched on smaller pieces
of cloth, black for the nose, pink for the cheeks, and red
for the mouth. She had tied the cloth over one end of the
ear of corn, then made a bonnet to go over that. Pulling

the husks only halfway down, she had tied a cloth skirt over them. They made delightful, rustly petticoats, which Mother said sounded like the taffeta ones fine ladies wore in the cities back east. She had rolled cornhusks tightly and covered them with cloth, then tied them on for arms. She had made a percale dress with a real button and button-hole and a sash that tied around the waist.

For Christmas Phoebe had made Araminta the dearest scarlet coat out of scraps of the old petticoat Mother was making over for Phoebe. All in all Araminta was one of the most elegant and certainly one of the most beloved members of the Dawson family.

Martha was still crying, wailing for "Ma-ma," but as Phoebe held her and sang, the wail quieted into almost a sleepy little song, and Phoebe decided that it was bedtime. She poured warm water from the teakettle into the wash-pan, unbuttoned Martha's dress, and washed her face and neck and arms, being careful not to wet her petticoat and shirt. She hung Martha's long flannel nightgown on a hook in front of the fire, and when it was toasty warm she slipped it onto the child. Next, she unbuttoned the high black shoes, took off the long black stockings, and slid Martha's long drawers and shirt and petticoat off all at once, as Mother had taught her. That way no draft hit her. Last of all, Phoebe set the pan of water on the floor and let Martha step into it, wiggling her toes in the water while Phoebe washed and rinsed her legs. Martha grew so interested in making little spatters with her toes that she forgot to cry. And shortly she was tucked in her own warmed blanket, like a little island in the middle of the Big Bed.

The Big Bed was the one built against the wall, where Mother and Father slept with Martha. It had a wooden framework on three sides with canvas strips to hold the big feather bed.

Under the Big Bed was the trundle bed, only slightly smaller. It was made on small wheels, and at night was pulled or "trundled" out into the middle of the room. The three boys slept in it.

Phoebe and Tessie had narrow beds, one built above the other, against the side wall. But tonight Phoebe said: "Tessie, shall we sleep in the Big Bed with Martha? She won't want to be alone."

As Martha always went to sleep long before Mother and Father went to bed, she found nothing unusual in being in bed alone, and in fact was even now almost asleep. But Phoebe did not want to sleep alone tonight, and no more did Tessie, so they agreed to keep Martha company, although neither mentioned her real reason.

Phoebe dreaded mentioning bed to the little boys, who were now absorbed in watching Hartley make a long cabin of their corncobs. But when she suggested that their eyes were drooping, Hartley came to the rescue.

"If everyone is in bed by the time I think it up, I'll tell a story," he announced.

Tessie quickly slipped into her nightgown and plumped into bed beside sleeping Martha. Gently she reached out to hold one of Martha's hands. Phoebe and Hartley pulled out the trundle bed. David and Robbie, with only some mild shoving and wrangling, hurried into their long night-shirts and into the bed almost before it was ready.

Theirs was no feather bed, but a ticking stuffed tight with straw. It was lumpy but on the whole quite comfortable for two tired little boys. They stretched out with their arms folded under their heads, rejoicing to be safely in before Hartley had finished thinking up the story.

Phoebe moved the cradle close to herself, glad that Mary Ann was not fretful. "I do hope she doesn't wake tonight," she confided to Hartley.

The boys began to clamor for their story and Hartley launched into a tale of Pecos Bill and his horse, Widow-maker. By the end of the story Tessie and David and Robbie were asleep. They were sure Hartley and Phoebe would take care of them. But the two oldest felt strange and uneasy.

Hartley whispered cautiously, "Phoebe?"

"Yes?"

"Are you asleep?"

"No."

"I was thinking — they could be back in the morning. One of them, or even both."

"Yes, they could," she agreed. There was a little silence. "Hartley?"

"Yes?"

Phoebe said reluctantly, not really wanting to say it, and

yet not able to resist, "Of course — there's no doubt they will get back — safely."

Hartley was quiet a moment before he answered. "We must trust the good God, Phoebe, as they do."

"Yes, I know. I do. But I wish they would come soon."

"We could say, 'The Lord is my shepherd.' "

Phoebe began, and Hartley joined with her, softly in the darkening room,

"The Lord is my shepherd, I shall not want. He maketh me to lie down in green pastures; He leadeth me beside the still waters. He restoreth my soul; He leadeth me in the paths of righteousness for his name's sake. Yea, though I walk through the valley of the shadow of death, I will fear no evil, for thou art with me; Thy rod and thy staff they comfort me. Thou preparest a table before me in the presence of mine enemies; Thou anointest my head with oil; my cup runneth over. Surely goodness and mercy shall follow me all the days of my life, and I will dwell in the house of the Lord for ever."

As they finished, there came again the howl of a hungry coyote far out across the snow-crusted prairie. Phoebe saw Hartley put an arm around the sleeping David, even as she cuddled Tessie close to her. She had thought she would never, never, never go to sleep this night. But she did.

CHAPTER 3

PHOEBE WAS AWAKENED BY THE BABY'S FRETTING CRIES. She snuggled deeper into the soft, warm feather bed and wondered drowsily why Mother was so long in taking Mary Ann — then she jerked wide awake.

Mother is not here! Phoebe remembered. The cold light of dawn was making its way through the windows; the coyote's howl had given place to the thin crowing of the roosters. The room was cold. Phoebe's nose told her so, and she longed for Father to be building up a roaring fire, and Mother settling the baby and starting breakfast and getting the day off to a cheery beginning.

"Wa-a-ah!" cried Mary Ann more loudly. Phoebe made herself face the situation. No one would make a fire until she did.

"I have to get up," she told herself. "I am responsible. I must!"

It was not easy, but once she started she slid out quickly so she would not let any cold air in on the other girls. As she got really awake her conscience began to hurt her about the baby. How long had she been crying?

"Sh, sh, Mary Ann. Sister's coming," Phoebe crooned. Her fingers raced, buttoning buttons, fastening hooks and eyes, and tying strings, so that she was dressed in a twinkling. With her foot she set the cradle rocking while she hastily cleared away the ashes of the burned-out fire, and began another. The baby must be fed first. Then breakfast for the others, and clearing up — the day's chores seemed to stretch ahead endlessly.

Long as they seemed, however, the hours of the morning did go by with the familiar routine of cooking, washing dishes, smoothing up the beds, sweeping the floor, bringing in water and fuel, cooking and washing dishes again. But by afternoon all the children were tired and fretful. Phoebe and Hartley quarreled over whose job it was to empty the slop pail, the boys whined to go outdoors to play, Martha would not take her nap and cried for mama. Tessie wanted Mary Ann, and Mary Ann fussed to go to Phoebe, until they were all wailing at once, and Phoebe thought she would scream. Hartley had won his argument by going outdoors and leaving them.

"Oh, Mother, do come home!" Phoebe pleaded almost out loud. "You've been gone forever."

"No, boys. For the last time, you know Mother said you can't go out because you have had croup. And if you don't behave yourselves I'll lock you in the storeroom."

But the boys only wailed louder than ever at this threat, and as Phoebe knew she would not lock them in the storeroom, she wished she had kept still.

Finally when Tessie had given up trying to get Mary Ann

to come to her, she pulled Martha aside and began to whisper to her. Martha slowly stopped crying to listen. She put her finger in her mouth and nodded in agreement, although she still sobbed a little once in a while. Then Tessie got out the precious Araminta and put her into Martha's arms. Martha looked and felt and patted, because usually she was not allowed to touch Araminta. Then she kissed the doll's painted face, and held up her own face for Tessie to kiss.

Tessie whispered to Phoebe, "Could I rock her in the cradle? I'll take her shoes off and play she's my baby. For Mary Ann isn't using it. Please?" she pleaded.

The cradle was large, quite large enough for even a three-year-old.

"Very well, if she will let you I don't see why not," Phoebe decided.

"Martha," said Tessie coaxingly, "want to play baby, and Tessie rock you in Mary Ann's cradle? See how nice," Tessie rocked it invitingly.

Phoebe expected Martha to refuse, but instead she said firmly, "Not Mary Ann's cradle. Martha's cradle," and plunged in head first.

"Oh, dear, wait, your shoes! You'll get the nice bed all dirty!" Tessie protested. So Martha hung her legs over the side, and Tessie unbuttoned the high-top shoes. Then she happily tucked Martha into the comforts and sang "Rock-a-bye, baby, in the tree top," as she gently rocked the cradle back and forth. Phoebe sat in the big chair and cuddled

Mary Ann, and gradually David and Robbie, for want of an audience, settled down to whittling listlessly.

Phoebe had expected Martha to stay still less time than it had taken to get her shoes off, and that any moment she would pop out again. But after a few wiggles she was very still, and when Tessie finally tiptoed around to look at her, Martha was sound asleep! Tessie was delighted. Finally Mary Ann, too, went to sleep nuzzled into Phoebe's neck. Putting her carefully in the middle of the Big Bed Phoebe told Tessie, "You were certainly a fine helper, getting Martha to sleep like that. I don't know what I would have done, for Mary Ann never would have slept in all that hubbub."

Tessie beamed and whispered loudly to the boys to hush, because her baby was asleep, too.

Just then the snow crunched outside the door, and they all four dashed over shouting, "Mama!"

But it was only Hartley.

When he flung himself out of the house after his quarrel with Phoebe, he had persuaded himself that the Stephens girl's horse needed exercise, and had ridden it down across the open prairie. He never even admitted to himself that he was looking for his mother, but he just happened to go south as far as he could keep a good view of their windmill for a landmark. He just happened to turn around in the saddle watching toward the south, long after he had turned his horse's nose back toward the north to go home. He thought again and again that he saw some dark spot growing, but each time it turned out to be nothing but a cloud or his own imagination.

Because he was so intently watching the south horizon, he was almost at home again before he noticed the heavy clouds blowing down from the north. They were black and tumbling fast, and Hartley suddenly realized that the air was getting thick, and the wind had grown hard and sharp.

"A storm!" he exclaimed and his heart sank. A heavy, sudden snowstorm was treacherous; he no longer hoped his mother had started home, but prayed fervently that she had not. More than one traveler had perished in a prairie storm only a mile or so from shelter.

Meanwhile he had no time to lose, for the evening chores were still to be done, and the darkness was closing in fast. He urged the pony to its fastest gait, leaped off quickly, and only stopped to knot the bridle reins around the manger post in the barn before he raced for the house — to be greeted by the eager children who rushed to welcome their mother.

"Phoebe," Hartley panted, short of breath from his run and from the excitement, "there's a storm coming. Almost here. I just noticed. Get the rope, and I'll go start chores."

The rope was a piece that would reach from the house to the barn, fastened to a wooden hasp at each end. It was used as a guide during a blinding, thick storm, so they would not get lost in the vague whiteness. The rope hung in coils on a hook at the side of the tall dish cupboard.

Phoebe could not quite reach it. Quickly she swung David up. He grabbed the rope.

"Hartley," Phoebe said, "you take this end and go on. I'll tie the other one here."

"Don't let it slip loose," Hartley called, even as he ran, unrolling the rope behind him.

"I won't. See, I have it caught now," Phoebe called after him. She gave the end of the rope twist after twist around the iron prongs. It must not come loose.

"All right on this end," came Hartley's voice.

Phoebe, who had not waited to put on wraps, ran back into the sod house to warm herself by the fireplace. But she thought uneasily of all the important things Hartley had to do. She had felt the snow in the air. It would not be long.

"Tessie," she said suddenly, "could you possibly stay with the little ones while I help Hartley?"

Tessie's eyes were eager. "Oh, yes! Yes, I could, Phoebe. I'd be so careful!"

Phoebe was already pulling on overshoes, bundling into her heavy jacket, and tying a wool scarf over the cap.

"Keep them out of the fire, and don't let the fire go out. If you get hungry you can have bread and milk. If the storm catches us, Hartley and I must stay safe in the barn perhaps, so if we are slow getting back you must not worry. I think we will be back quickly, but for no reason must one of you open that door. Understand?"

All three nodded solemnly, and Phoebe darted out, running toward the barn. As she sped across the dooryard, the first snowflake hit her nose. The wind blew so hard it almost carried her. Facing into the wind, as they would be when they came back, she and Hartley would be glad of the rope to help pull themselves along, even if the snow did not blot out the sight of the house.

Hartley's face reflected his anxiety as he worked fast forking hay in for the cows and horse. He was glad to have Phoebe with him.

"But what about the children?"

Phoebe explained, while she sat down by Bessie with the milk pail.

"Good little Tessie. And she's always been so afraid of her own shadow," Hartley said approvingly.

"I'll milk while you get in the fuel. Better get plenty, if there is time."

"Yes," agreed Hartley, not wasting breath from his work. At a run he fed and watered the chickens, gathered up the eggs and took them and a basket of cobs to the house.

"Children are fine," he called to Phoebe as he came running back to refill the basket. He could not see her, but he could hear the steady squirt, squirt of the milk into the pail.

"How's the snow?"

"Worse, but not thick. I think we will make it."

Hartley took two more baskets of cobs in. Then he filled the water barrel; he filled the extra pail with water and set it in the storeroom. The wind was fierce, now, and there was little light, but he still could see the outline of the

They made their way along the taut rope

soddy, and the faint glow of the firelight through the windows.

When all the stock had been fed and watered, and Phoebe had finished milking, she and Hartley stuffed hay into the cracks by the barn door where the wind was drifting snow in. Then Phoebe with the milk pail and Hartley with the last basket of cobs made their way along the taut rope to the door of their home.

They each paused at the door to look once more off to the south. But the thickening snow in the dusk cut off the view so they could hardly see beyond their own barn. Neither spoke their thoughts as they stamped the snow from their boots, brushed their shoulders as best they could, and went in to the warmth of the house.

They had been gone only a short time, but the boys flung upon them as though it had been months.

Tessie said proudly, "I took care of them all," and Martha echoed, "I took care of them all," not particularly knowing or caring what she was talking about.

"Well, at least, Hartley, we have done all we can, and we are safe and snug for the night."

"I was thinking, Phoebe," Hartley confided, "the storm must have been coming up for a long time. I just hadn't paid attention, but they would have, both of them; they would be watching the weather, and even if they were out, they would find shelter — or something," he finished weakly, picturing to himself how little shelter there was between their house and that unknown one to the south.

"I'm sure they would neither one start out with this

kind of weather coming," Phoebe assured him, although she was far from feeling assured herself.

Her throat was so tight she thought she could not possibly eat any supper, but she must get it for the others. She cooked grits with ham, made gravy, and heated sauerkraut. With applesauce made from dried apples, and bread and milk, it was a good meal, and Phoebe discovered, once she sat down to the table, she was eating almost as much as usual. But she dreaded the evening ahead, as the wind whistled mournfully and the fears for her parents kept coming back.

"I know what let's do, Phoebe," said Hartley suddenly. "After supper, let's have a party."

"A party?"

"Yes, a party. We could pop some corn, and crack some of those hickory nuts . . ."

"And make some taffy," Phoebe entered in enthusiastically. "There's plenty of molasses. Tonight we can't just — just sit here. A party will be the very thing."

"And we'll play Poor Pussy, won't we?" asked Robbie, clapping his hands. He flung gravy from the spoon he was holding all over David and Tessie, but Phoebe wiped it off as best she could without bothering to scold. Anything to keep them happy, this night.

"Phoebe," said Tessie, "I can wash the dishes, just like you do, so you can get started on the party."

"Yes! And Davie and me will wipe, won't we, Davie? We'll both wipe together."

"Oh, no. You'd be sure to drop them, and then where would we be?"

"No, we wouldn't either, would we, Davie? We could stand and hold them over the table. And then we'd have the party quicker."

"Well, I suppose, if you're so determined."

"Phoebe," asked Tessie, as she importantly got out the dishpans, "can Martha and Mary Ann come to the party, too?"

"Martha come party!" that one said at once.

"Yes, I think Martha can come, because she took a good nap. But Mary Ann is too little, so first I must wash her and put her to bed."

"And then you'll make the party?"

"And then I'll make the party. Here, pet, I'll pour the hot water. We can't have you getting burned. But you can do all the rest, every licking bit if you want to."

Hartley brought out the nuts and the molasses and popcorn. After Phoebe had the dishwashing crew set up, she poured molasses into a big pan and set it over the hottest part of the fire to boil. While it heated she covered the bottom of the iron skillet with yellow grains of popcorn, which she and Hartley themselves had helped hoe and husk. She fastened on the special cover Father had made, with holes in it, and began gently shaking it over the coals.

Hartley joined the dish crew to put things away, and to empty the water. Then he brought the two big stones they kept for cracking nuts. He cracked the nuts while

David and Robbie and Tessie began picking out the meats and Martha began eating.

"Here, you little squirrel, keep out or we'll never get ahead," Hartley told her, but he laughed as he spoke. Martha laughed, too, and went on eating. The others ate a good many nut meats in the process, and the little bowl did not seem to fill very fast.

"Now look, you fellows," Hartley finally exclaimed impatiently, "stop eating, or we'll never get any ready."

"Well, Hartley, all we're going to do is eat them. It's not like getting them ready for cookies or anything, so why not just let them eat them?"

"All right, sure. And the party can begin right now!"

Robbie came to Phoebe and tucked a nut into her mouth. "Here's a big one for you, Phoebe, because you aren't getting any, and the party has already started," he said.

And then they heard — *Pop!* and then *Pop-pop!*

"It's popping!" all the children screamed at once. And so it was! *Pop! Pop-poppety-poppety-pop-pop-pop!*

Phoebe shook the skillet, the corn rattled and popped until it sounded like artillery fire, and then all was quiet.

"It's done! Put in the salt and the butter, Phoebe, it's done," they yelled.

Phoebe carried the skillet to the table, but as she took off the lid to pour out the corn — *Poppetypop-pop* suddenly went some late ones, and they bounced corn all over the room, including some right on Phoebe's nose.

How they all laughed and laughed! Then the molasses began to boil, and Phoebe stirred it so it would not burn, and began holding up the spoon to see how the syrup dropped off. At first it ran like water. Then it got thicker and slower and thicker and slower — then a tiny thread hung down and Phoebe said it was done.

Everyone shouted to everyone else, "Stand back! Out of the way, she's going to pour it." Phoebe carefully wrapped the handle of the pan with pot holders and poured the bubbling syrup out into the big stoneware platter Tessie had greased.

"Now we'll play a game while it cools," Phoebe said.

"Pussy Wants a Corner," demanded David.

"Poor Pussy," shouted Robbie.

"Fruit Basket Upset," yelled Tessie.

"I know," decided Phoebe, "we'll let Hartley shut his eyes, turn him around, and let him point. And the one he points to will have his game."

Hartley squinched his eyes, so that even David was satisfied he was not peeking, and Phoebe turned him around and around. Then she arranged the children in a line.

"Now," she signaled.

Hartley pointed, and opened his eyes as the shout went up, "Robbie gets it."

"I get mine. It's Poor Pussy."

So Robbie started as the pussy, and mewed and purred beside Phoebe, who was able to keep perfectly serious as she patted his head and said, "Poor pussy! Poor pussy!" Then he tried Tessie, and she did not laugh, either. But Martha laughed and mewed with him, so she was it. Martha loved being pussy. She crawled on her hands and knees, and mewed so piteously and purred so vigorously that even Hartley, who usually was hard to get, laughed right out loud.

When they had each had a turn, they played Fruit Basket Upset, and then Pussy Wants a Corner. And at last Phoebe announced, after several gingerly tests, "Candy's ready to pull."

"Whoops!" shouted the boys, forgetting all about corners for lost cats.

"Wash good, and grease your hands," Phoebe directed.

What a sudsing there was then, and what a scurry to wipe on the roller towel, and to rub butter all over their hands. Then Phoebe, pulling the sticky mass into smaller hunks, gave each one a gob to pull. Even Martha had a tiny ball which she rolled around and around for a while between the palms of her hands, and then tucked into her mouth.

"I'm going to put some nuts in mine, may I, Phoebe?" asked Tessie.

"Oh, yes, that's good. And do see how pretty Hartley's is getting. He is really pulling it."

David dropped his once, but Phoebe did not see, so he picked it up, dusted it off a bit and pulled it some more. As the candy began to stiffen too much to pull, Phoebe helped the children twist it into long, thin ropes. Then she used the big scissors, dipped in water, to cut off little pieces, letting them drop back onto the platter. Hartley had pulled his so hard and fast it was a creamy, delicious color. The others were darker brown, but they all tasted wonderful.

When they finally washed the sticky off their hands and the worst off their clothes, everyone was getting a little tired. Presently David, flopping down on the Big Chair, discovered that curled up in the soft sheepskin lining, sound asleep, was Martha. She did not even blink as Hartley and Phoebe quietly took off her shoes and stockings and dress and tucked her into bed right in her underwear.

"Phoebe, we aren't sleepy, are we, David?" Robbie cried, fearing that Martha's collapse would give Phoebe ideas. "The party isn't over yet, is it?"

"What we might do is to get all ready for bed, and I'll spread a buffalo robe on the floor right here in front of the fire, and we'll poke the fire up and put some more wood on, and then we'll all cuddle up together and tell continued stories."

"Oh, Phoebe, I just love continued stories," Tessie said, although she broke into a yawn in the middle of her words. "And I've got a real, good exciting part all ready."

"Don't make it too exciting, Tess," said Hartley, and Phoebe glanced at him in understanding. So he had not been able to forget the storm howling outside, either!

But the children were eager for the rest of the party, and the boys were ready for bed almost painlessly. Then they settled, one in each of Phoebe's arms, while Tessie sat between Hartley's legs. The candy and popcorn and nuts were put within easy reach of them all, and they watched the sparks from the hedge wood pop out of the fire with merry little crackles.

Now if only Mother and Father would walk in, how

perfect it would be, thought Phoebe. She began the continued story safely with a family that had a big house, and a great big kitchen just for cooking, and one day they had a lot of company from back east who came to stay for a long time. This led to many rather dull incidents, when she turned it over to Hartley, who added a fast Indian pony for each of the children. He was interrupted to decide on the colors and names of all the ponies, and by the time it was the turn of the younger ones to add chapters, they forgot the great adventures they had planned, and soon finished with everyone having a big barbecue.

Even the boys made no protest about bed. They were asleep almost before they were in bed.

While they had all been laughing and shouting they had drowned out the moan of the wind and the howl of the coyotes. But now as everything grew quiet inside, the storm outside sounded in all its fury. Phoebe and Hartley could only hope that neither Mother nor Father was battling through that wind and snow tonight.

CHAPTER 4

SOME TIME LATER PHOEBE AWAKENED, WITH HARTLEY'S hand on her shoulder. He was whispering, "Phoebe! Phoebe! Wake up!"

"What is it?"

"Listen!"

Startled, she sat up quickly.

"Hear it?"

"Yes," she whispered.

No one could help hearing. Someone was pounding loudly on the door.

"Mother or Father would not knock," she said.

"You didn't prop the door shut or anything?"

"No, of course not. And anyway, they would call if they couldn't get in, if it was them."

"Who can it be?" Hartley asked anxiously. For answer Phoebe merely shook her head.

"What shall we do, Phoebe?"

More than anything else, Phoebe wanted to crawl under the covers and shut her eyes and have someone take care

49

of her. But there was no one to do it. She was in charge, and she must decide.

Meanwhile, as they whispered, the knocking continued. Suddenly there was the whinny of a horse.

"We have to open the door, for if they were enemies they could come right in anyway," Phoebe whispered to Hartley.

"And it might be a messenger from them — or one of them — and if we don't answer, they might think it was a mistake and go away."

Hartley nodded in agreement. Phoebe, during the last speech, had been pulling on her stockings and shoes, and wrapping her jacket around her.

"You take the gun and cover the door. I will open it and stand behind it. Make them tell who they are and raise their hands. And I'll have the poker ready."

Again Hartley nodded, and moved quietly for the gun.

"Make your voice as deep as you can," Phoebe told him, "so they will know there is a man here."

Hartley's shoulders straightened and he took the gun with a firm grip. Phoebe was older, he thought, and in charge; but she was right, he was the man of the family. He slipped quietly into position, checked the gun, cocked it. He nodded to his sister, who lifted the latch and pulled the door open, stepping behind it as she did, and grasping the heavy iron poker ready against the wall.

"Raise your hands and tell your name and business," Hartley commanded sternly. He made his voice as deep as he could. Unfortunately it squeaked in the middle of his

"Make your voice as deep as you can."

speech. At the same time they heard a baby's thin wail, and a woman's voice saying, "Baby sick. Snow bad. Baby cold."

The dim figure they could see in the doorway stood motionless. The wild wind whipped snow flurries into the soddy. Hartley, startled by the unexpected sounds, dropped the point of his gun barrel. Then he remembered that it might be a trick.

"Come in," he said again, and Phoebe pulled the woman forward, still facing the pointed gun. Phoebe closed the door and anchored the poker across it to form a bar, in case others were outside. Only then did Hartley lower the gun. The woman, however, seemed to pay no attention to it. She repeated:

"Baby sick. Snow bad," and squatted by the fire, beginning to unwrap the bundle tied into her blanket. The baby cried feebly, and then gasped with the piercing "whoop" which Phoebe and Hartley recognized. The Indian baby had the same sickness that Robbie and David and Martha and Mary Ann had had. They knew about croup!

The mother seemed hardly to know what she was doing. She squatted still, rocking the baby in her arms helplessly as it coughed and choked for breath. Hartley, without a word from Phoebe, stirred up the fire and heaped on fuel. He swung the teakettle over the center.

Phoebe, meanwhile, by gestures and a few words managed to persuade the Indian mother to let her take the baby. Hartley, at her direction, brought clean, dry clothes of Mary Ann's and warmed them. The Indian mother's big, solemn eyes noticed the baby in the cradle, and she nodded understandingly when they brought out the clothes. In a very few minutes the change was made.

As Phoebe finished wrapping the baby warmly, Hartley lifted Mary Ann gently and tucked her, still sleeping soundly, into the feather bed beside Tessie. As soon as the cradle was empty, Phoebe put the Indian baby in it. With the quickness of much practice she covered the top of the cradle, hood and all, with a heavy blanket so that only a small hole was left under a flap at the top.

With the tongs Hartley lifted one of the stones loose in the bottom of the fireplace and laid it in the long-handled skillet. Then while he held the skillet inside the hole in the blanket, Phoebe carefully poured just a dash of water onto the stone, and quickly held the blanket flap shut so that the steam would not escape. Again and again they did it, until the rock no longer sizzled.

Hartley quickly changed the stone, putting that one back to heat again and another hot one in its place, and they repeated the steaming process. Gradually but surely the whooping was less intense, the baby breathed more easily. Phoebe stopped long enough to wrap several hot stones in old cloths and lay them in the ends and sides of the cradle.

Then they made more steam, until Hartley and Phoebe grew so tired they thought they could not move. But they kept at their job faithfully until at last the wheezing, although hoarse, became regular. The baby had gone to sleep!

All this time the mother had crouched, motionless, watching them, making no sound. They gestured her to come look. She peered into the covered nest where her baby lay, and then nodded slowly. She still said nothing.

"She looks tired," Phoebe whispered to her brother.

"She's probably hungry. Shall we offer her something to eat?"

"Oh, yes. I'll get something."

Phoebe lighted a candle at the fire and went in to the storeroom to bring out the last of the corn bread, and a piece of cooked ham and some milk. She offered the food to the young woman, who seemed to wake up when she saw it. She took it in both hands and ate eagerly.

Phoebe poured hot water from the teakettle into three mugs, added molasses and milk, and gave one mug to the visitor while she and Hartley each had one. The drink was warm and soothing, and Phoebe and Hartley relaxed from their excitement and labor and sipped their mugs cozily before the fire. Phoebe glanced up at the mother, to discover that she was nodding, sleeping sitting up with her cup still in her hands.

"Poor thing, she's terribly tired. I'm going to watch the baby, and let her sleep," Phoebe announced. She bent over the woman and touched her. The woman was awake at once, and glanced at the cradle, now almost quiet. Phoebe motioned toward her own single bunk, empty, and made it clear that the visitor should sleep on it.

But the young mother shook her head. She pointed to the baby, then to herself, laid her head on her hands and closed her eyes and then shook her head again violently. She would not leave the baby. She would not sleep. She made it quite plain.

Then Phoebe, making signs, urged that she would watch the baby. She opened her eyes wide to show she was not sleepy. No, she would not go back to bed, she would sit right there by the cradle while the mother slept.

Finally the mother yielded, but something still was bothering her. At last they understood — her horse! They had forgotten all about it!

Hartley by now was warm with the hot milk and very tired and sleepy. His brothers looked so cozy in the good old trundle bed. He longed to be in with them, wanting nothing in the world less than to finish dressing and go out in the wind and snow. The horse had been left too long already. Probably it had made a long, hard journey, judging from the condition of the rider.

But Hartley said nothing of all this and silently began to pull on overshoes. Phoebe, who was not watching him, listened for him to offer to take care of the horse. Someone must. The woman could hardly do it herself in a strange place. Phoebe wondered if she, herself, should. Certainly she could not make Hartley do it if he didn't want to. And then she heard him stamp his foot down into his overshoe. She whirled around, to make sure. He was almost ready.

"Oh, Hartley! You're going!" she exclaimed.

"Well, sure," he said grouchily. "If you had any sense at all, you'd know a horse can't stand in that wind after a hard ride. Lucky if it isn't ruined already. Just like a girl. What they don't know!" He stamped out sullenly.

When he returned he found the visitor already asleep in Phoebe's bunk, the baby still wheezing but sleeping, and Phoebe just refilling the teakettle.

Hartley was not sullen or tired now. He was wide awake and excited. "Glory, what a horse! Oh, Phoebe, you should just see him! He's as big as any horse I ever saw, and walks like a dancer. I think he's white, he just looked like a solid shadow against the snow. Oh, wait until morning. I wiped him good, and gave him hay and some of the oats . . ."

"Oats! But there are so few left!"

"Phoebe, I tell you he's beautiful!"

"I suppose that makes him need oats more, even though they are nearly gone."

"Oh, girls! They just don't appreciate a good horse!"

"I guess I want a horse just as much as you do, but that doesn't have anything to do with running out of oats for the work horses just before spring plowing. Anyway, I suppose that much won't make any real difference."

"In the morning I'm going to ride him. The snow is letting up, it's almost stopped, but it is drifting bad. The Indian won't be able to leave for a long time, probably."

"You hope."

"Well, you wouldn't send a sick baby like that out again in the cold. Oh, Phoebe, do you suppose I'll ever in my life have a horse like that?"

"No," said Phoebe practically, "nor me, either, for you know those fast Indian ponies cost ever so much. They are no good for heavy pulling and farm work, and Father needs a new team of work horses, and all sorts of important things. But I do think maybe, some day, he will get us another riding horse better than Captain."

"Oh, Captain!" Hartley dismissed him contemptuously. "I mean a real horse! Some day I'm going to, somehow."

"There's no sense fretting for what you can't have. Here's a piece of candy left, want it? And you might as well get back to bed."

"I'm not sleepy now. I'll stay up with you."

"No, you'd better go to bed. You will be sleepy when you get there, and one of us will need to be rested tomorrow. Hartley, I think the mother is sick, too. I felt her hand. She is awfully hot."

"The baby seems better."

"It's sleeping, and Mother always thought it was good when the children slept. But listen how hard it breathes!"

"Maybe we should do more steam?"

"I'm dreadfully tired. And I know you are, too. But I think maybe we'd better."

So they made more steam again several times, and then, when it was almost time to get up, Hartley once again pulled off his clothes and lay down in the trundle bed.

Phoebe wrapped a blanket around her shoulders and settled into the Big Chair with the cradle at her feet. She was sure she would not sleep deeply that way but would waken if the baby began to breathe hard and choke again.

Of course when the other children woke in the morning they were amazed to find a new little brown baby in the cradle. They recognized what the blanket over the top meant, and all said to each other, "Poor baby is sick!"

Now Tessie was in her element with two babies to help with, for the mother was indeed sick. Although she insisted on getting up, she soon saw that her baby was well cared for, and let herself be coaxed back to bed. She took the baby into bed with her to nurse it, and then let Tessie put it back into the cradle. Tessie rocked it, and then held Mary Ann, so that Phoebe could work.

The Indian mother had only a few English words, but Phoebe and Hartley finally made her understand, by pictures drawn on the hearthstone with soot, and many gestures, that their mother and father were coming soon.

With all the other things to do, Phoebe had to bake corn bread and churn butter. She boiled beans and cabbage and salt pork, and made cottage cheese from the sour milk.

There seemed to be children under her feet every step she took, and she was so tired she thought, long before she was through, that she could not make another move. But somehow, finally, they had all gathered around the table and had a good dinner; the dishes were washed, and then Phoebe tumbled into bed with Martha for a nap, leaving Hartley to watch the little boys and Tessie to take care of the babies.

Hartley had indeed had a good ride on the wonderful horse; in the daylight it turned out to be a golden palomino, and Phoebe drifted off to sleep as Hartley described it over and over again, every detail, to an audience that was as eager as he was.

Phoebe awoke feeling much better. She was further cheered by Hartley's announcement that the storm had cleared, the wind was gone and the sun was out, warm and springlike. The Indian mother got up again, seeming much stronger. She went to the door, looked around at the weather, and then indicated that Hartley should bring her horse.

"But you can't go yet!" Phoebe and Hartley both protested. Hartley motioned to the baby, and then coughed horribly and shook his head. But the mother insisted on the horse, so Hartley reluctantly went to get it. However, she made no preparations to leave, but sat by the cradle quietly looking at her baby. When the horse nickered outside the door, she left the baby where it was and went out.

"Is she going to leave us the baby?" asked Tessie hopefully. Phoebe also wondered for a moment, and then knew she couldn't, as the baby was still nursing. Anyway the woman had not put on her own jacket, nor taken her blanket. Phoebe went to the door to see.

The horse was, indeed, beautiful. Except for a creamy white mane and tail it was a pale-gold color. It pranced even standing still.

Hartley obviously hated to slide down. The woman made a surprised noise as she saw Hartley and the horse. The horse nosed her and she patted him, looking at him carefully, then nodding approval. Perhaps she had just worried, and wanted to know that the horse was all right after the bad night.

Now she was twisting his mane, and then Phoebe saw that she was braiding into it a loop of beads she had been wearing. She braided the hair tightly and tied the end in a firm knot. She looped the reins together on the horse's neck. Then she stepped back, and suddenly swatted him on his flank. At the same time she gave a loud, piercing yell, another and another.

The great horse seemed to dance uncertainly in the same spot for a moment. Then he was off like a fast golden bullet disappearing into the southwest. In the late afternoon sunshine he seemed like one more sunbeam.

"Whatever did she do that for?" wondered Phoebe.

"Probably she is sure he will go home. Maybe they belong near here," Hartley suggested. "No one could find them after the snow, but now that the wind is down and the snow is crusting on top, it won't drift any more, and the horse could easily be tracked back. It wouldn't even take Indians to do that."

The Indian woman, who had stood shading her eyes with her hand, watching the disappearing stallion, turned to them now.

"Man come." She pointed to herself, and said again, "Man come." She started back into the house. Again in the house she knelt by her baby, felt of it carefully and put her ear near its chest. It was breathing much more quietly, and waving its hands happily. She sat in the Big Chair, and it nursed fairly well, choking and whimpering only occasionally. This was the first time the children had

had a good look at it, Phoebe had kept it so covered in the cradle. Now they were entranced by its beady, black eyes and solemn frown.

By the time she had fed the baby, the mother looked very tired again. She tried to help Phoebe, but as she was not accustomed to things in their house, and as Phoebe could talk to her so little, she could not do much. Phoebe urged her to lie down again.

Hartley came in with the evening's milk and eggs. Phoebe fed them all coddled eggs and cold corn bread and cheese. She had filled the dishpan and the drain pan before the children finished, she was so eager to get the dishes done and get to bed.

The Indian mother went back to Phoebe's bunk, but she took her baby with her, so Phoebe once more tucked Mary Ann into her own cradle. She let Tessie rock it while Phoebe undressed Martha.

The boys protested, "Why, Phoebe! It isn't bedtime! It's still light!"

"It's getting toward summer so it stays light longer. Anyway we are going to bed now, so don't let me hear another word out of you two," Phoebe exploded.

"Phoebe's awful cross," Robbie said to Hartley who had just brought more fuel. He turned to look at Phoebe — and saw her on her knees, undressing Martha — and two big tears falling down her face.

"Phoebe!" he exclaimed, alarmed. He ran to her, "Are you sick?"

"No, I'm not sick!" she said.

"Well, what is the matter?"

"Robbie told you. I'm cross. I'm just cross. I'm so cross I can't stand it, and if one more thing goes wrong . . ." She yanked at the sleeve of Martha's nightgown, which had somehow got tangled inside out. She could not see clearly for the tears which kept filling her eyes. Hartley looked at her for a moment, then reached for Martha, who was whimpering impatiently in her petticoat.

"Here, rabbit, you come to Hartley."

"No," she drew back petulantly. "Phoebe."

But Hartley picked her up anyway.

"Phoebe has to go to bed. I am going to dress you, and don't you squawk or I will eat your feet."

"Phoebe go to bed?"

"Yes, Phoebe go to bed now."

"Phoebe sick?"

"No."

"Phoebe bad girl?"

By now Phoebe was laughing through her tears, and saying, "Oh, Hartley, I'm all right. I didn't mean to be such a goose, and you have done lots, too. Give her here. I'll finish."

But Hartley, looking for all the world like their father, stamped his foot and pointed. He said in his deepest voice (which, now that it did not matter, did not squeak), "Young lady, are you going to do as I tell you, or not?"

Phoebe giggled. Martha peered interestedly, the little boys crowded around big eyed. Tessie threatened to storm in protection of Phoebe, until Phoebe winked at her and smiled, and she understood that it was a game. Martha clucked sympathetically,

"Oh, oh. Too bad. Phoebe naughty girl. Tsk. Tsk."

Phoebe laughed indeed then, as did all the others just because she did. Hartley tossed Martha high, and began untangling Martha's gown. Phoebe thanked him, pulled off her clothes, scrambled into bed, and was asleep almost before she got there.

Phoebe had gone to bed first! Before anyone except Mary Ann! It was quite amazing to all the others, even to Hartley who found his new imitation of Father very useful as he sternly sent the boys to wash and undress, and cuddled Martha until she was asleep before he laid her down, so she would not disturb Phoebe.

"Hartley," said Tessie, "see, I'm all ready for bed, and no one told me." And sure enough, she was!

"Tessie, you are a super splendid young woman, and when I am ordering children, I will order them all just exactly like you," her big brother told her. "And what's more, I'll make Araminta a little house of her own, because you have been such a good girl. Just see if I don't."

"Will it be a soddy? A little baby soddy?"

"Oh, no, a frame house like our new one. There will be scraps I can use."

"I'd rather have a soddy, just like our own home."

Hartley laughed. "Well, it will be your house, so it will be whatever you want."

"I want a soddy. A little soddy just big enough for Araminta and all the babies she is going to have." Tessie beamed happily, and kissed him shyly, and he gave her a good bear hug, as near like Father's as he could make it, not having rough whiskers on his chin to rub into her neck. Then Tessie kissed Martha, and then, because Phoebe didn't, she kissed David and Robbie, who submitted gracefully although ordinarily they did not care much for kissing.

Hartley thought, as he tucked Martha in and took off his own shoes, "This is our third night alone! And this is really easier than the first. Why, what if they did not come for a week? We can manage perfectly well."

CHAPTER 5

THE NEXT DAY DAWNED CLEAR AND STILL AND MUCH warmer. The snow was beginning to thaw, making it sticky and good to pack. Phoebe sent Tessie out to play a while, and then, leaving her and the Indian woman to look after the children, she went out for a short while herself.

My, how good it was to get out in the bright sun, and to run and jump and yell. No wonder the little boys and Martha were fretful, after their weeks of being shut up. Phoebe resolved to be very patient with them, and to make up to Hartley for his help the night before.

The sun was so warm now that Phoebe believed Mother would have let them out a little, if she were home. But Phoebe dared not take a chance. So she and Hartley built a snow horse and rider, and Hartley put on a real rope bridle. Then they made a little dogie calf to be chased. She wrapped the children, one at a time, in a big blanket and carried them to the doorway to look at it.

When she came in Phoebe brought a great pan of fresh snow. She quickly dipped it out into dishes, set out the molasses jug and the cream pitcher, and they all feasted on mushy ice cream of mixed snow, syrup and cream.

The Indian mother ate hers and smacked her lips to show that it was good. She gave some to her baby, who liked it and wanted more. So Phoebe gave some to Mary Ann, who was bigger than the Indian baby. But Mary Ann was not certain whether she liked it or not. She rolled it on her tongue, spit it out, then reached for more. Martha tried to feed her some and nearly stuck a spoon in her eye. The whole crowd, Indian mother and all, watched her intently and enjoyed the ice cream and the snow.

That was why, undoubtedly, they did not hear the door open. Phoebe was suddenly so frightened she almost dropped Mary Ann. She saw a huge Indian standing right behind Hartley. He had not come in, she was sure. He was just there!

She was too startled to scream, but she caught her breath. Hartley, opposite her, looked up. She knew by the expression on his face that there must be another Indian just behind her. But the Indian she was watching was paying attention only to the Indian baby and its mother. The Indian woman had seen them. As Phoebe looked up frightened, the woman began talking, quite rapidly, and at times pointed to Hartley and to Phoebe, and once to the cradle.

All the Dawsons had been at first too surprised to say anything or to move. But their general fear of strangers and their particular fear of Indians — at least of Indians who were neither babies nor mothers — drove the young children to cling to the older two when their first shock was over.

The little soddy was now bulging with people. When

Phoebe gathered courage to look around, she saw there were four Indian men.

She told herself they would surely be grateful for the help given the mother and baby. But the men stood so solemn and silent and stern she wondered whether they might be angry at the woman herself. Even if they were not, perhaps she would not have any influence over them. But what could Phoebe do? Or Hartley?

Phoebe caught his eye, and Hartley shrugged his shoulders helplessly. Both shrank from making a move, for fear it should be a wrong one. Hartley held Tessie and David, one in each arm. Phoebe was holding Mary Ann, with Martha crowded close beside her and Robbie hugging her neck firmly. And they all stared silently. The Dawsons stared in fear at each other and the Indians. The Indians stared curiously at the Dawsons. Hartley glanced once toward the gun, but he immediately thought better of it. The only sound in the room was the voice of the Indian mother and the occasional reply of the man she was talking to.

Phoebe watched his face intently. She was trying to decide whether he looked friendly or cruel, and how he felt about what the woman was telling him.

Then the quiet murmur was broken by a deep, ringing voice which brought all the little Dawsons to their feet.

"Chief Flying Hawk! You are welcome to my home, you and your people. But isn't this a little crowded?"

"Father! Oh, Father!" the little Dawsons shouted at the first sound of his voice. They rushed upon him in a

The Dawsons stared in fear

stampede. Chief Flying Hawk seemed as startled by the arrival of Mr. Dawson as the children had been by his. But he was obviously neither frightened nor angry. Solemnly he greeted Mr. Dawson.

"Chief Flying Hawk is grateful for the kindness of the family of his friend," he said. "My son's wife and her son had been to visit the people of her family across the Cottonwood River, while my son and others were away trapping. The baby was sick, and she sent word she would stay longer. So we did not look for her.

"But the baby was better, she started home and was caught by the storm. Her horse is very good, but he could not find the right path in the storm. After much riding she saw the lights of your windows, and came. Your children made her welcome, and made my grandson better. For this, the tribe of Flying Hawk will be forever grateful, and these," he spread his arms to include all the intent children, "will be as members of our tribe for now and for all time."

"But where is your mother?" Mr. Dawson asked the children, who talked all at once, explaining to him what had happened. He held them closer to him, his arms reaching on both sides, as he began to understand something of what they had been through. But he remained calm and dignified, just as the Indian chief was. He answered the chief as though such a thing were a mere trifle, a thing he took for granted.

"We are honored," he said, "to have you or your family as our guests at any time. Even though my wife and I should happen to be away, these young people (he did not even call them children) represent us in offering the hospitality of the prairie. Please consider our home open to you and your people."

Phoebe thought he did it grandly, and Hartley wriggled in pride. Then, while the men finished their conversation and the young mother wrapped her baby and herself, he slipped outside to see if the beautiful golden horse was there.

Sure enough, there it stood, not even tied. Several more Indians lounged around on horseback, and held the horses of those who were inside.

Back of them, circling around the dooryard, were the long-awaited wagons filled with boards and nails for the new house and barn. Hartley's past experience told him there would probably be goodies and special presents, too.

Ordinarily all of these things would have excited him, but now he was hardly aware of them. He had eyes only for the golden beauty, his friend. He stepped up to the palomino. An old Indian on a brown and white pinto near by, holding the bridle of another palomino, spoke sharply as Hartley approached the big horse.

"Boy, no — horse bite, kick. Only squaw ride."

A couple of other Indians moved closer, but Hartley had no fear of them. For sitting, watching behind them, were the drivers of his father's wagons. They did not know, any more than Mr. Dawson had when he drove up, what was the meaning of all these Indians in the dooryard.

The Indians seemed peaceful enough, but the drivers

watched, alert. They seemed casual, but Hartley guessed they would produce guns in a hurry if any trouble started. Besides, his father was at home! Hartley was not afraid of anything!

So when the Indian told him that only the woman could ride the big golden horse, he felt he must show off. He had already ridden it. It never occurred to him that the palomino might be any less friendly now. He spoke to the horse, and then with a swift movement he caught the silky mane in his right hand, gave a leap, and was once more astride the broad, golden back.

The Indians gave a cry of terror. The horse could be very fierce, and they really expected that it would not only throw but possibly turn and kill the strange rider. But they were helpless, for the horse and boy were off like a flash of light.

The yells of the Indians were followed by shouts from the drivers, not sure what the excitement was. Mr. Dawson and the chief dashed out of the door in alarm. At a glance the chief saw what had happened, and leaping onto his own horse, almost a twin of the other, he was off to follow.

Two of the other Indians had also ridden after the boy. The old Indian at the doorway explained to Mr. Dawson that not even the chief's horse could outrun the squaw's. But they might pick up the boy, after he was thrown, before the horse turned and trampled him.

Mr. Dawson ran for his gun and started on foot, with some idea of getting a shot at the horse. But the horse and boy were almost out of sight. And the other horsemen still followed.

One of the drivers had climbed the windmill. Now he shouted, "The boy is still on! Still a ridin'! And doin' all right, far's I can tell. I think they're a headin' back. Yep, he's a turnin' him, and here they come. They passed the Injuns, and they're a turnin'. Here they come! The big feller's skimmin' along like a wild duck, but gentle, seems like. The others are a high-tailin' it, but he's leavin' them way behind."

The Indian woman and Phoebe had come out, and the younger children all pushed through the door wanting Father. There was a big audience as Hartley came sailing back into the yard, sitting easily on the horse's broad back, and gently pulling him to a stop.

The palomino stood, quivering with eagerness, but not moving an inch. Hartley sat a moment patting and praising the horse, while his father set down his gun and the Indians and drivers all began exclaiming.

Mr. Dawson stepped over to hold the horse, but the palomino jerked his head and reared, and Mr. Dawson could not touch him. Hartley slid down reluctantly, still patting the smooth, golden neck as the chief rode up and leaped to the ground.

Phoebe had feared he might be angry, but instead he seemed very pleased. He put his hand on Hartley's shoulder, and nodded approvingly at him. Then he said to Mr. Dawson:

"You have a son to be proud of, my friend. He is a great

rider, for no man before has ridden the great Golden Chief. My son gave him as a colt to his wife, and he has been as a child of her own, but never before has he let another ride him. More than one has tried, and some who tried were injured before they could be rescued. No man of my tribe will try now to ride the Golden Chief, yet this one has made him as a young lamb. Truly he is a great horseman, although not yet a man of full years."

While the chief spoke, both Hartley and his father gloried in the praise, and Phoebe and the other children were very proud, too. However, Mr. Dawson could hardly understand how Hartley could have developed such skill. He had never ridden anything before more spirited than their old plow horses, or the gentle pony, Captain, who would safely carry Martha all around the dooryard for hours with no one else attending.

But when the chief at last finished his speech, the Indian woman said, "Boy good. Horse know." And then in her own language she explained to Flying Hawk, who in turn explained to Mr. Dawson and the drivers, that Hartley, in the middle of the night, had gone into the storm to care for the horse. The horse, she said, had become his friend and carried him gladly.

The chief and his men felt even better at this explanation, as it showed the smartness of Golden Chief. They valued a boy who would take such good care of a horse. Besides, it was pleasanter for them than to have to think that a mere boy who was not even an Indian was so skillful in taming the horse none of them could ride.

At last the Indians were ready, and the mother tied the baby into its blanket over her shoulder. Then, holding the baby in her left arm, she grasped the horse's mane and leaped upon his back as lightly as Hartley had done with no burden at all. It took down Hartley's pride a bit, and made Phoebe resolve to practice with Mary Ann on Captain.

When the mother and baby were settled, Chief Flying Hawk loosened the reins on his own horse, which seemed to leap into the air and dash off; the mother on her Golden Chief followed closely, with the rest of the men in a line behind.

The Dawsons watched until the file was small in the southwest, where they had watched the golden stallion disappear alone before.

"Well," said Mr. Dawson, as he lifted Martha to carry her back into the house, with the others following, "unless I miss my guess, you children have made yourselves some very good friends." Then he added to the drivers, "A man need not fear to pioneer in new country with such helpers as these."

The men all agreed, and Phoebe and Hartley knew that such praise they would remember all the rest of their lives.

Now Mr. Dawson petted the little ones, listened to their tales of their adventures, and heard all about the wonderful party and the cunning Indian baby and the corncob fence and cabin and the new house Araminta was to have, all of which seemed of about equal importance to them.

He sat in the Big Chair, with Mary Ann and Martha in each arm, Tessie between his knees, and the little boys on the back of the chair holding his hair. Most of them were talking at once, but their father listened and laughed and hugged them all at the same time.

Hartley was at the barn with the drivers, who were still bragging about him as the family went in. But Phoebe, who felt that tons of weight had fallen off her shoulders, sat on the children's bench, just enjoying looking at her father and assuring herself that he was really home.

"And now, daughter," he said after a bit, "do you suppose you could get us some dinner? I know you have had a great deal to do, but we have had a long trip since our breakfast. We didn't stop, and I promised the men a good home-cooked meal, once we got here. Of course I didn't dream what had been going on here, but if you could just sort of find something . . ."

"Of course, Father," and she jumped up. "The children will want their dinner, too."

"I really hate to ask you to do more, Phoebe."

"Oh, Father, I don't mind. It will be fun, especially now that you are home," she said.

"I'll help Phoebe," Tessie said, pulling away from her father.

"You?" he teased. "Why, you're no bigger than a rabbit. It was only the other day that you were the cradle baby, Tess."

Tessie stood straight and looked at him. "I helped

Phoebe, and I took care of the little children all my own self while Phoebe helped Hartley in the storm. Didn't I, Phoebe?"

"Indeed she did, Father. We never could have got along without Tessie. And when the boys fretted, and I was so exasperated — well, I'll tell you about it later. But you must know she is really quite a big girl now."

"Tessie bi-i-g girl," Martha announced. "Martha bi-i-g girl, too. Martha wipe a dishes. All a spoons." She nodded her head.

"And we wiped dishes, Robbie and me did," David claimed.

"Well, well! So you've all been growing up while my back was turned. And I suppose Mary Ann churned the butter, and we will have to get a new baby for the cradle."

At this they all laughed, even Mary Ann.

Then Phoebe and Tessie bustled around, and Martha toddled over to them, wanting to bustle, too. So Phoebe told Tessie to let her put the forks and spoons around.

Phoebe was determined not just to "sort of find something," but to have a real meal for her father and his men. She gave Tessie potatoes to bury in the coals of the fire. She fried thick slices of ham, and boiled cabbage, and made fried biscuits with wheat meal, because Father was home with new supplies and they need not save it any longer. The butter and cottage cheese were fresh from the day before, and there was applesauce left over, because she had made a lot.

She had Tessie set on dishes of pickles, and fill the sor-

ghum pitcher and the cream pitcher and the milk pitcher,
and Phoebe made up the last of the coffee in the storeroom.
At the last minute she poured cream into the skillet with
the ham grease to make gravy.

When Mr. Dawson called his drivers in from the barn,
he could indeed be proud of the meal set before them. The
men all said what a wonderful cook Phoebe was, and Mr.
Dawson thanked them. He said, putting his arm around shy
Tessie, "Both of my older daughters are very competent
little women, I am glad to say." Tessie actually giggled
out loud.

One of the men said, "I'm going to wait for her to finish
growing up and marry me, because I have been looking for
a long time for a wife who is such a neat, useful little body."

"What about it, Tessie?" Her father laughed.

Instead of hiding her face Tessie looked at the man and
said, "I'll see when I grow up if I like you or not."

Then all the men laughed, and her father patted her.
When he said, "A very good, honest, sensible answer,"
Tessie glowed.

When the men had eaten, they went back to the wagons
to unload. Then the children had their dinner together,
and talked of all the excitement they had had.

David said, "Hartley says there are ever so many packages in the wagons, and great big boards, and little barrels
with nails, and there will be scraps and crooked nails we
can make things with."

"When do you suppose Mama will get home?" Tessie
asked.

"Father thinks we will at least hear from her tomorrow," Phoebe told them, "because Mr. Stephens with two wagons was with the wagon train, and left them at the cut-off. If things are all right at home, he can manage, and if he still needs her he can send one of the men with a message."

"I think she'll be surprised to hear about the party and the Indian baby," Robbie said, and Phoebe was sure she would.

Once again Hartley spent his spare moments climbing the windmill to look for Mother or a messenger, but he had very few spare moments. There were many boxes and bundles to unload, and things to be carried to the storeroom, others to the barn, and extra water and fuel for Phoebe in the house because there were so many to cook for. Hartley thought he had never known anyone in the world could be as busy.

But there was no worry about it, for he need not plan or think or decide. And Hartley was so relieved to have a grownup at home again to take the responsibility that when his father told him to do something he never once protested, or asked why.

When the big covered wagon was empty, her father said to Phoebe, "I think some sun will do these little ones good. We will bundle them up and put them in the wagon. They can watch us work, and you can run about a bit."

Phoebe was indeed delighted, for she had been aching to watch the unloading, and supposed there was no chance at all. She put beans on to boil while she was out, because they would almost make a meal with the left-over corn bread and plenty of milk. And she frisked around over the piles of new wood, smelling it, and poking the bundles and wondering which one might be her own special present. When Mary Ann began to fret for her supper, Father carried her back in, cradle and all. Then he carried the others back across the snow. It was a great adventure to be out again, after the weeks cooped up in the same room, and they were all lively but tired when they went in.

Phoebe began the familiar process of washing and feeding and dressing the baby, and setting the table and cooking. Soon the drivers had been fed again and gone to the barn, where they would sleep on the hay. Then the Dawsons had their dinner, the dishes were finished, and Phoebe at last sat with her father before the fire, with the children again clustering around him. She had just begun to tell him her version of all that had happened when Robbie broke in, "I hear bells."

"Me too. I hear bells, too," David said.

Then they all heard bells, but before anyone could get to the door, it opened — and in came Mother!

What a scramble there was then! Everyone rushed to hug some piece of her, and Hartley shouted "no fair" when Father picked her up and held her, way high in the air to have first kiss.

"Oh, Francis — put me down," Mother protested, but she laughed, and he did as she said, for he had already had his share.

Then Mother let herself be led to the fire, and unwrapped, and she must pick up Mary Ann, sleeping though she was, and look at her carefully and say she had grown. Then she tucked Mary Ann in again and held Martha and kissed the others all around again. Then the little boys must sit on her lap. Martha went back to Father, and Tessie sat on his other knee to wait her turn with Mother. When they had finally settled, Mother suddenly remembered the Stephens' driver, who had driven her home in the sleigh and would stay the night in the barn and ride Marietta's horse home in the morning. She would have jumped up to find him, but Father pulled her back.

"The barn is full of men, and they have a campfire. There is no need to fret. They can look out for themselves for once."

So she sat back, and at last the children could begin to tell her of their adventures, of their worry in the storm for fear she might be on her way, alone.

"But I was not, you see. I was a little afraid for you, but not much, for I was sure you could be depended upon, although I certainly never expected, when I left, that I would be gone so long. But it is a good thing I went, for Mrs. Stephens was very sick."

"How is she now?" they asked.

"She is much better, although she is weak and must stay in bed for a long time. But her husband is home now. And what do you think we had for him when he got back?

"It was a new baby. The very littlest new baby boy anyone almost ever saw. But it waved its fists at him and yelled, just like a big boy."

"Oh, Mother," exclaimed Phoebe, "how dear. Was it sick?"

"I think it is all right now, dear, but it had hard work at first, it was so tiny. We wrapped it in wool and put hot stones in a little drawer to make a bed for it, because it was so much smaller than the cradle, it would have rattled around in it. And at first we could only feed it by dipping a clean cloth in warm milk and dripping it into its mouth.

"But today it was eating quite well, and Mr. Stephens is sending back to Westport for his sister to come out and help. I promised that Phoebe could come in a few days, after I got settled and you have had some rest, Phoebe dear, to help until the aunt gets here.

"And now," she went on, "tell me. Did you have any trouble from the storm? I see you have the rope up. That was thoughtful."

"Just wait, Mother! Just wait! You can't think what all happened," they broke in. She looked startled, then, because she had supposed all the time that nothing had happened, and Father leaned back, puffing his pipe, and grinning to think how surprised she was going to be. Then they all began to tell, and to explain, and tell some more, while their mother's eyes grew bigger and bigger.

Once the boys cried, "Mother! You're squeezing us," as she got so excited she almost hugged them in two when Phoebe and Hartley told of their opening the door, and of Hartley getting the gun, and Phoebe grabbing the poker. She interrupted to "oh" and "ah" at times, and to approve with a "that was the right thing" when they told of steaming the baby, and on and on clear to Hartley's last adventure on the beautiful palomino, and the praise of Chief Flying Hawk.

One by one, the younger children dropped off to sleep, and Father tucked Martha and Tessie into bed, then pulled out the trundle bed and lifted the boys in. Mother picked up Mary Ann once more, just to reassure herself once again that there was not a trace of fever, and that her cheeks were filling out.

Phoebe was half expecting her father to say, "Well, youngsters, time for bed," as he usually did. But instead he built up the fire and filled his pipe, and said, "You know, Marian, there's some chocolate in the box in the storeroom, and a big sack of sugar. Seems to me this would be a good time for a cup of hot cocoa."

Mother exclaimed, "The very thing, Francis," and she and Phoebe had some steaming in short order. They all four sat back before the fire, Mother and Phoebe in the Big Chair, Father and Hartley on the buffalo robe on the floor. Like four grownups they drank their chocolate and talked everything over again. Mother was interested in just what they had had to eat, and whether they had enough sleep. Phoebe told about Tessie's skill in distracting the boys when they started crying, the first night, and Hartley told her in great detail all about the beautiful palomino the Indian woman had.

At last there was a little silence, and then Father, looking into his empty cup, said thoughtfully, "I guess you thought that was a pretty fine horse."

"Oh, Father, he was magnificent! Riding him was just like flying!" Hartley was excited all over again, just thinking of it.

"I know you would like one, son. Of course, not like that, but at least a good, spirited riding horse. And Phoebe, too. I had hoped that perhaps this year we could get a good horse you could both use. Now that there is to be a school next winter, I want you to go. But you know the new house and barn will set us back a good deal, and we must have a new team of work horses if we are to farm that east eighty; I just don't see how we can make it this year."

"Oh, Father," Phoebe exclaimed, "I told him so. We didn't think of it, not really."

Hartley said, "Nobody had to tell me! I've got that much sense. And as for school, Captain can take us in the buggy, and Tessie too, for she's old enough and she's going to be real grownup before long."

Mother's eyes watered. She gave Phoebe a sudden hug, and then she hugged Hartley, and then kissed her husband and slid down to lean against him.

"You see, Francis," she said, "I told you all the time you didn't need to worry about them. Phoebe and Hartley are not tenderfeet. They understand that we must have a bigger house, and horses for the farm work, and a place to put them. We have so much more than we used to, but we must do each thing in turn and be grateful for what we have."

Her husband kissed her and said, "Right you are. And we do have a lot to be thankful for, with boards right here for a fine house and barn, and such a fine pack of children to put into a new house. Come, let's all go to bed, for tomorrow is another day, and at any rate, there are some packages in the freight I think you'll want to see. You've made us all so proud of you."

Never had her old straw tick felt so good to Phoebe as now, when she stretched out and pulled up her comforts, knowing that she had not a care in the world. For Mother and Father were back in the Big Bed, God was in His heaven, and the prairies were peaceful and serene.

CHAPTER 6

WHEN PHOEBE AWOKE THE NEXT MORNING, SHE DIS-
covered that the little ones were already dressed and beginning to poke and pry into the treasure boxes. She had slept
right through all the early morning clatter. Now the room
was warm, the baby was gurgling happily, and Mother
was making a big pot of cocoa, and boiling coffee, and
frying eggs and biscuits.

"Good morning, sleepyhead," Mother greeted her cheer-
ily. "You're about to miss your breakfast."

"Oh, Mother, it's such luxury to wake up and not have
everything ahead to do myself," she said.

Mother laughed. "I should guess it was. But it is a
luxury you have earned. Hartley is just up. He can't wait
to get his hands on some boards and nails. But you can
stay as long as you feel like it."

"I'll be up in a jiffy to help you. My goodness, Mother,
I never realized how much you have to do, and I didn't
do any washing, or ironing, or sewing! I don't see how you
get it all done. I am going to help more, just you see!"

Phoebe was dressing quickly as she talked, and soon had the table set and the children washed and combed.

They all felt how good it was to be together again, all around the table, with Father in his own place asking the blessing. When he added a special prayer of thanksgiving they all of them said "Amen" with all their hearts.

After breakfast came the opening of the boxes. There were bolts of cloth for underwear, and yarn to be knit for stockings, and pieces for shirts and dresses. There was a pair of store pants for Hartley, and shoes for them all, and any number of other supplies, tools and spices and harness snaps. And there was a doll for Martha, a real store doll, which Tessie eyed wistfully until another, just like it but larger, was discovered for her. For each of the boys there was a jackknife, and a beautiful necklace of blue stones for Phoebe. There were packages of flower seeds for Mother, who wanted a flower garden in front of the new house.

All of them exclaimed over their treasures, while Father smoked his pipe and asked Mother again and again if the piece goods was what she wanted. She insisted she could not have done better if she could have gone herself, except that he really should have got a better quality flannel for his own shirts.

Phoebe pranced around the room with her necklace over her old brown Mother Hubbard, and thought how beautiful she would feel when she had on the new blue dress which Mother had promised to make with a very full skirt and ruffles on the neck. "I don't think I could stand any more happiness right now," she said.

Then they opened the boxes

The spring days began to come in earnest, although in between there would be occasional cold, driving rains that saturated the sod of the roof and started steady, monotonous little drips here and there through holes which the field mice had made.

For Mother and Phoebe it made extra work, as they had to move the bedding and empty the pans set out to catch the water. But the children thought it was pleasantly exciting. When Mother was not looking, the boys would stand under a drip until it wet their hair and began to run down onto their clothes. And Father said, "Well, Hartley, at least this year we won't have to patch the roof. By fall, if all goes well, we'll have a shingle roof over our heads."

No one ever really minded rain, even though it meant being cooped up indoors a good deal of the time, for even the little ones knew that rain meant promise of good crops.

Hartley plowed with the old team and the sulky plow, and Father drove a new, rather restless team with a gang plow which turned over two furrows at once. As soon as the ground was dry enough that the horses' hoofs didn't sink down and pack it, and the plowshares would cut the soil without collecting mud, Dad and Hartley began at dawn and worked until dark. First they plowed the garden, about five acres, south of the windmill. The land there sloped a trifle, and if the season was dry, as so often it was, the Dawsons could pump water into the garden and raise food when the other crops burned up.

The garden was Mother's, and she was always impatient to get it in. Father insisted nothing grew as long as the ground was cold, but Mother wanted potatoes planted by St. Patrick's Day. This year, on March sixteenth, Father brought the pails of carefully selected seed potatoes from the storeroom out to the sunny grass south of the house and called, "Well, Marian, get your knife and help cut potatoes if you want to get them into the ground tomorrow."

His eyes twinkled and he winked at the children, although his voice was gruff. That was the first Mother knew the garden would be ready, and she was delighted. She left the sewing she had started, and she and Phoebe cut potatoes while Father and Hartley started plowing the eighty acres to the west, where they would plant corn.

Mother squatted down, her full skirts making a circle around her in the dried stubble and the new soft spring grass, and began deftly cutting potatoes and singing.

The potatoes had begun to sprout with the coming of spring, and each one must be cut so as to get as many chunks as possible, each with a healthy sprout. There must also be enough potato left on the sprout to feed it until it got a good start in the ground. It took skill to do it well.

Phoebe was trying to learn, but she kept coming out with sprouts that had no potato, and hunks of potato with no sprouts. As the sprouts, or eyes, were the live part, of course without them the piece of potato would not grow. Phoebe grew discouraged, and then she watched Mother's fingers moving swiftly and surely. She would determine again to learn to do it as well. Long before the job was finished her fingers were cramping, and she had cut herself in several places; nevertheless, she stuck it out and was pleased to discover that the last ones somehow came out better.

For the Dawsons, the first planting was always a rather special ceremony. Every member of the family helped, even little Mary Ann, who was only beginning to walk, and wanted to put the nice, soft, black dirt in her mouth.

The sun was warm but the constant wind was sharp, and Mother insisted that everyone be buttoned snugly into jackets or sweaters. The cut potatoes were in four buckets, one for Mother, one for Phoebe and Tessie, one for the little boys and a small one for Martha. Father carried Mary Ann, and led the procession; then came Mother carrying her potatoes, and Martha with hers, then the girls, the little boys, and Hartley with several hoes marching at the rear. Father's high tenor rang out, and Mother's soft alto joined in, and then all the children, some on key and some not but all singing loudly,

> "We plough the fields and scatter
> The good seed on the land,
> But it is fed and watered
> By God's almighty hand.
> All good gifts around us
> Are sent from heaven above;
> Then thank the Lord,
> O, thank the Lord
> For all his love." *

* From *Pilgrim Hymnal.*

Verse after verse they sang, until they reached the black-brown line of newly plowed dirt. There they set their potato buckets in a circle. Then the family joined hands in a circle and Father made a special prayer.

Originally, when Father and Mother had first come, it had been a natural impulse for them to stop to pray on the edge of the first little piece of broken sod from which they hoped so much. And to prevent the little Hartley and Phoebe from getting lost in the high, thick prairie grass, Mother had held one, and Father the other by the hand. Year by year the tradition had grown. This year Father's prayer was largely one of thanksgiving.

"Our loving Heavenly Father," he began, "we thank Thee for bringing us to another time of planting, when it is our privilege to share in Thy miracle of growth and increase. We have received Thy loving bounty so that we have had food for our bodies; we have received the blessing of these additions to our circle. Help them to gain in knowledge of Thee as they grow up. Grant that in the coming year we may all use Thy gift of life to further Thy kingdom of love. Amen."

Mother whispered to Martha, "Now!"

Martha responded to her cue, picked up one potato piece and gave it to Mary Ann.

Mary Ann was eager to taste it; the little boys giggled, but Tessie, who had been trying for days to teach the baby to be ready for this moment, coached her excitedly, "Plant it, Mary Ann! Plant the potato!"

Mary Ann looked around at the watching, loving faces,

and recognized an audience. She held the potato to her
mouth but only stuck out the tip of her tongue to taste,
and then bent double to push the small ball into the dirt,
pushing it as deep as one small finger would go.

"Aw panted." She smiled, very pleased with herself, and
her father scooped her up for a kiss. Then Martha planted
one, and the little boys and Tessie, and the work began in
earnest. All but Father and Hartley walked along the rows
dropping potatoes at regular intervals. Father and Hartley
began pulling the dirt over with their hoes, being careful to
get neither too much nor too little. Besides the potatoes,
there were onions and beans and peas. Mother liked to
start them early in small patches in hopes they might escape
a late frost.

"I always feel so much better when I know things have
started growing again," she exclaimed with satisfaction as
she and Phoebe took the little girls back to the soddy and
started to fry ham and eggs.

Spring was the time when so many things needed attention. Phoebe did not see how she could be spared to go to
the Stephenses. There were new lambs to be watched for,
setting hens to be shut up in nests safe from weasels and
coyotes while they hatched their eggs. Hartley was working
long days at the plowing, so he could not do all his usual
chores, and of course the housework always went on.

"Mother, I simply don't see how you can spare me,"
Phoebe said earnestly. Mrs. Dawson smiled and kissed her.

"Remember, Tessie is getting bigger, and the little boys
can begin helping more with the stock. We'll have to man-

age, I think, because Marietta will be even busier than we are, and I am afraid her mother will not be very strong for a while."

Somehow, in spite of all the other things to be done, Mother squeezed in some time to sew. At night she hung blankets to shield the children's beds from the light of the coal-oil lamp, and as Phoebe drifted off to sleep she heard the steady thumpety-thumpety-thumpety-thumpety of the sewing-machine treadle. In the morning there was a new, white cotton-flannel nightgown for Phoebe.

The second day after the planting, Father was to drive Phoebe six miles east to get the stage which would take her to within two miles of the Stephenses. From there it would be easy to walk, for the Stephens' cabin was right on the little stream which the stage forded. All Phoebe need do was walk west on the south side of the river until she arrived.

Thoughts of going alone, on a stagecoach, off into strange country to visit strange people made Phoebe feel very much as she felt at the prospect of climbing the windmill. But again, she would have died rather than let anyone know her qualms and call her "tenderfoot." Almost before she knew it, her freshly starched and ironed petticoats were sliding over her head, Mother was fitting the top on the lunch basket, and Father was testing the straps that secured the big leather telescope that held her clothes. Then Hartley drove the wagon up to the door and yelled in brotherly fashion: "No use primping for the stage driver, he's an old married man with three children."

"Oh, Hartley!" Phoebe was indignant, but Mother and Father just laughed.

"Now, have a good time, dear, and I know you'll be a help to Marietta. Don't lose your pocketbook, Daddy will give your fare to the driver, and your return money is sewed inside the belt of your under-petticoat. Give it to Mrs. Stephens when you get there to keep for you. Don't start eating your lunch until you are sure the motion of the stage isn't going to make you sick. Have you got your handkerchief?"

Yes, she had it, a lovely, thin piece of white which one of her aunts back east had sent. With it, she was a real young lady, and of course much too grown-up to be homesick, or to forget all the ways a lady should behave.

The stage took much longer than usual to reach Phoebe's destination because it was spring freshet time. Many places which were just dips in the prairie the rest of the year were now wide, rushing streams that had to be forded at carefully selected spots. It was all exciting, and Phoebe soon forgot to be homesick as she became interested in the changing landscape. But she was more than a little relieved, as the driver told her, "This here is Osage Ford, ma'am," and pulled his horses to a stop, to hear a man's voice call: "Hello, driver! That little girl come for the Stephenses?"

"Yep, here she be, Captain, only she's no great shakes as a little girl; she's right smart of a growed-up young lady." He added politely to Phoebe, as he set her telescope down, "And here's yer gear, ma'am."

Marietta's father was a huge man with a booming voice,

but he was very friendly. He asked Phoebe if she could ride astride, as he had brought horses but had no sidesaddle. Phoebe was embarrassed, but decided not to pretend.

"I never rode any other way. We haven't any sidesaddle, although Mother tied some old ropes to the crib in the barn to make stirrups, and fixed a pad of grain sacks and showed me how to sit."

Mr. Stephens laughed and boosted her up into a big cow pony saddle.

"Your feet are too short for the stirrups, but hold onto the horn and Tony will take you home."

He fastened what the driver called her gear behind his own saddle, and led the way along the edge of a strip of big trees, much bigger trees than Phoebe had ever seen before.

The Stephens' home was a log cabin, or rather two log cabins, each about twelve by eighteen feet, with a sort of connecting porch, open on the south, between the two. The double house had been the idea of the three big boys of the family, older than Marietta, who had gone back to Westport to work for the winter. With two houses, they said, the older folks could have company without keeping the younger children awake or being run over by them. Marietta heard the horses and voices and opened the door of the east house, calling such a cordial welcome that Phoebe knew she was not really among strangers.

This side was used for cooking and eating and general household tasks, and the other house, or room, was ordinarily where they all slept. Now Marietta's mother had a bed in the corner of the general room, so that she could supervise the family and yet rest part of the time.

Beside her bed was a woven baby basket hanging by leather straps from the rafters. It had been bought from Indians in the Southwest by one of the big brothers and brought home to the Tiny One, as they called the new baby, the tenth child in the family. It was a splendid arrangement, Phoebe could see at once, as it kept the baby off the floor away from drafts and out of reach of the toddling and scuffling brothers and sisters who seemed to be everywhere at once.

Mrs. Stephens was a pretty woman with fluffy, honey-colored hair and a slow voice. She kissed Phoebe, to her surprise, and thanked her for coming.

"And here," Mrs. Stephens went on proudly, "is our little Marion. We named him for your mother, you know." She turned back the knitted shawl for Phoebe to look.

Mother had warned Phoebe that the baby was not pretty yet, because he had been born too soon. But Phoebe was not prepared to see such a hideous little creature.

She was shocked and thought to herself, "He looks like a sort of shriveled peanut with a pig's face! How awful for them — and the rest of the family are all so good-looking." She was embarrassed, not knowing how to console them, and thinking of the sad contrast between this and her own beautiful, chubby-cheeked Mary Ann. She was thinking, Oh, you poor, poor people, when Mrs. Stephens asked, "Isn't he a darling? But then, we've been lucky that way, all our babies have been lovely — at least to start with," she added, smiling and pinching the cheek of a middle-sized brother who had pushed in.

Phoebe thought she could not have heard right, and was so surprised she turned to stare at Mrs. Stephens. But the mother was smiling and intent on the ugly, red, wrinkled face in the basket. Phoebe cautiously looked at the others — at Marietta, at the father who was taking off his boots by the fire. Both were smiling with pleasure and satisfaction. Phoebe realized something new right then. Of course he is beautiful to them. He belongs to them.

Following her own thoughts, she added, out loud, "Really he belongs to me, too, partly."

The father said, "He isn't very big to divide among so many, but I reckon while we're dividing, you've sure got a right to a good share."

The strange thing was that as Phoebe looked back once more at the mite of a human being sleeping peacefully in his swinging nest, he had somehow improved noticeably in the seconds that had passed.

Wide, cottonwood planks had been laid over the rafters of the cabin to form a shallow loft which could be entered through a hole left open in one corner. Narrow boards nailed across the corner of the wall formed a ladder by which it was easy to climb up, and Marietta told Phoebe that they were to have the loft all to themselves while Phoebe was there.

At her invitation Phoebe climbed up far enough to look into the dim recesses. In the corner she could see a pallet of buffalo skins covered with blankets, and spread neatly with sheets and more blankets. It looked irresistibly snug and private, and Phoebe could hardly wait until supper had been served and eaten, the evening chores finished, and she could retreat to that inviting nook with Marietta.

Although Phoebe worked hard helping, life at the Stephenses was so different that the time raced by. The Stephenses were not homesteaders, like her own parents. They had bought their land, and they had many of the little comforts of life that money could buy. There were braided rag carpets on the floor, and glass windows, and a stove to cook on. The river furnished delicious fish, and the big brother who had come home killed a steady supply of partridges and pheasants.

Even the work seemed more interesting because Phoebe was not used to it. She went with the children to guard against their getting too near the water when they went to hunt for wild lettuce and sorrel along the banks. The Stephenses had a large herd of cattle, and were buying more. These had to be herded by the children, and often Marietta sent Phoebe out to take them sandwiches and a jug of buttermilk and sometimes gingerbread in the middle of the afternoon.

"If they know someone may come," Marietta explained, "they aren't nearly so likely to get into mischief, and a little extra food keeps them from getting too tired so they are cross and worry Mother when they come in at night."

There were twins, a boy and a girl, a little past nine,

and a boy a year younger but just as big. They were always together, working, playing or fighting. The girl's hair was cut short like her brothers', and she dressed just as they did, so that Phoebe at first could not tell any of them apart. They were called "the children" as distinguished from "the little ones," girls of three and four, and now, of course, there was Marion, "the tiny one." Phoebe was impressed by the way Marietta was in charge of the whole family, even of "the boys," the three older brothers who were at home for a day or two at a time and then left again to buy or trade cattle.

Phoebe, of course, understood that the mother was not supposed to do heavy work for a while, but that did not explain why Marietta did all the planning and managing, scolded the younger ones and decided what to have her father buy when he went to town. Then, one day, Mr. Stephens referred to something as having happened "when Marietta's mother was alive," and Phoebe discovered that this Mrs. Stephens was really Marietta's stepmother.

Phoebe knew the story of Cinderella, and she felt deeply sorry for poor Marietta, who had to work so hard to take care of her stepmother's children. She began to resent the pretty woman who cuddled her babies while Marietta washed their clothes, and who so casually left the table to sit in her rocking chair and sing and embroider while Marietta cleared and washed the dishes and then washed the children for bed. Phoebe found it increasingly hard to be polite to her, and she tried more than ever to help Marietta.

One day the two girls were turning and airing the straw

mattresses in the sleeping cabin and putting on the clean sheets they had washed in the river and then dried and bleached on the grass.

"There now," Marietta said, "you've been working hard all day, and you must be tired. Why don't you take the little ones out to play in the sun a bit? You can sit in the grass and rest. They will stay near you, and Mother can have some quiet while I get supper started."

Phoebe burst out, "I should think she could at least look after them. It isn't hard work and she goes out walking. You've been working all day, and you never rest or play or anything. I think she's mean!"

To her amazement, Marietta grabbed her shoulders and shook her as she sometimes did one of the children when they had been particularly exasperating.

"Phoebe Dawson, don't you ever again say anything like that about my mother. Never! Do you hear?"

Phoebe began to cry. She suddenly felt terribly alone and far away from her own mother and home.

"I didn't mean any harm," she sobbed, "but she isn't your mother, and — and I just felt sorry because she makes you do everything and you never have any fun. And I want to go home!"

Marietta melted as quickly as she had flared up. She put her arms around Phoebe and kissed her.

"Don't cry, dear. I'm sorry. I know you didn't mean any harm. I guess you don't understand. She really is my mother, even though she isn't my first one.

"You see, Phoebe, I can't remember my first mother. I

was a baby when she died, and all the time I was little there was just Father and my big brothers. They were all nice to me, they loved me and bought me treats, but the boys seemed almost grown up to me. We lived in a big house in Virginia, and Father hired different people to come in and do the work, but they kept changing, and no one really seemed to belong to me. I hadn't anyone to play with, and I was so lonesome. I used to sit at the window with my dolls and wish they would come to life and talk to me. They didn't, of course, and I would cry and cry.

"And then one day Father came home with a pretty young woman, and said 'Look here, daughter, I've brought you a mother. Joyce, this is Marietta.' And she laughed, so soft and pretty, and just put her arms around me and kissed me. And after that — well, you just can't understand how different life was. She was always there, when the others were gone. She sang to me, and taught me games, and played doll with me, and we had tea parties. I was a big girl, nine years old, but she would hold me on her lap and rock me as long as I wanted, and tell me stories, like she does now to the little girls.

"When the twins were born, and then the others, it was as though my dolls really had come to life at last. Mother always let me take care of them, and called them my babies, and they would come to me as quickly as they would to her.

"And then, times were getting bad back home, and Father and the boys thought there was a better future out west. Yet Father hesitated to bring Mother because she

had always been used to having things nice; but she said if
he thought it was best to come, she was willing and would
try her best.

"We went to Iowa for two years, but things didn't work
out there, and she lost a baby, and was sick, and yet all the
time she is sweet and cheerful — just like you have seen
her. And you see, Phoebe, I'm strong and healthy, and I
love keeping house, and having babies around to do things
for, and seeing them all so happy and full of fun and never
knowing what it means to be lonesome. Really, Phoebe, I
love every minute of the day, especially when I remember,
sometimes, how I used to feel. And I'm so glad I can help
make things easier for her. I'm just grateful every day of
my life that I have such a sweet mother to do things for.
Now — forget I shook you, will you please? I'm sorry, I just
did it before I thought."

The girls kissed each other and went, together, to get
supper. But all the rest of her visit Phoebe saw the family
in quite a different light, and she thought again and again
of how much she herself had taken for granted. She realized
that she, too, was glad to have a mother to do things for,
and that it was going to be nice to be home again.

By the time Marietta's aunt arrived, tiny Marion was
almost six weeks old, and was beginning to look like a human
baby. The cottonwood trees had come into bloom and filled
the air with their fluffy white blossoms. All the Stephenses
exclaimed again and again at how much it reminded them
of "back home," when the real cotton was in bloom. The
aunt, Phoebe soon saw, knew less about housekeeping than

even the mother did, and would mostly mean one more person for Marietta to take care of. But Phoebe no longer pitied Marietta, who enjoyed life so thoroughly. Phoebe had come to believe that Marietta could do anything in the world.

One of the big boys, Christopher, offered to drive Phoebe home with a wagonload of split wood which the Stephenses were sending as a thank you to the Dawsons. The return trip was a new adventure as Christopher had been to college in the east, and all the way he told Phoebe fascinating stories about the beginnings of America, and Virginia, the state where he was born. He spoke of the different kinds of pioneers who had pushed farther and farther west, until at last Phoebe was amazed to hear the names of the Dawsons and the Stephenses as part of the people who were making history.

This gave Phoebe a great deal to tell Hartley and the rest of the family. When at last she stood in the dooryard of the familiar soddy she could hardly wait to begin. But Phoebe had still more to think about, and she was astonished at how different everything seemed after only four weeks.

CHAPTER 7

WHEN PHOEBE AND CHRISTOPHER HAD ARRIVED IT WAS TOO dark to see much outdoors, and Phoebe had been too eager to get back with the family to think of anything else. Christopher was to stay for the night. After the younger children had finally calmed down and slept, Phoebe had a cozy visit with her mother while Christopher and Father and Hartley sat outdoors and talked.

But the next morning's light was hardly penetrating the deep recesses of the windows when Hartley was impatiently pulling at Phoebe, urging her to come out to see the surprise. She woke quickly, excited to realize that she was at home again, and followed his lead up the windmill.

"What do you see?" he asked excitedly.

Below her the prairie stretched in a checkerboard of squares and rectangles of different colors — the waving, yellow green of the forty acres of wheat, the wispy green stripes that marked the rows of young corn showing in the brown earth of the corn field, the deeper green of the prairie grass, and below them the variety of long rows that was the garden. All of these were familiar sights, and Phoebe so enjoyed seeing them again that it was a long moment before she saw what was different.

"A wagon!" she exclaimed. To the northwest, not more than a mile away, was a Conestoga wagon, with a line of clothes flapping in the wind.

"Neighbors!" Hartley told her. "Name is Pfitzer. They talk Dutch but the father knows a little English, and there are five boys, two just about my age."

"No girls?" Phoebe's disappointment was keen. They had always longed for close neighbors, and after her visit with Marietta she more than ever wished for another girl.

"No girls — there. But look east."

Incredulous, Phoebe saw, then, perhaps two miles off, a soddy — a new, rather large soddy with what was unmistakably smoke curling from the chimney.

"They are Moores. They're from across the ocean, and they have eight children, most of them little, but the two oldest girls are a little older than you are. They're lots of fun, all of them. Father and I went over to help them build their house, and they know all kinds of new games. They talk funny, but I could understand them after I got used to it."

"Oh, Hartley, isn't it wonderful? Just think — two families so close we can see them."

"You know what, Phoebe? When the Moores stopped here, and said they were homesteading, Mother cried. She could hardly get over having another woman within walking distance."

Phoebe longed to go at once to get acquainted with the

girls, but that must wait for the present. Hartley had something else to show. Father had laid out the lines for the house, and a distant neighbor who was a stonemason was to come today to begin laying the foundation. In another week, a number of neighbors were coming for the day, to help raise the framework. As the women and children came, too, it would be a big social occasion. Mother would need lots of help to get ready. Phoebe heard in her mind Marietta exclaiming, "I'm so grateful to have a sweet mother to do things for!" and she determined that she would not even ask to go visit the Moores until Mother suggested it.

Mother was glad to have Phoebe take over for a while in the house so that she could catch up with her garden. There were still things to plant — late beans, and beets, and new lettuce, and cabbage plants to set out. Mother liked to do much of the early hoeing herself. So today Phoebe churned and made butter, cleaned the coal-oil lamps, and sifted corn meal with the big, wooden-rimmed shaker sieve to get out the hulls, so that they could make extra corn bread quickly. The children needed little care this time of year. They were outdoors most of the time, and it was only necessary to watch that they didn't climb around the windmill or fall into the tank.

In the late afternoon, Phoebe was helping the little boys look for a hen who had stolen her nest out. Just as she had climbed to the top of the straw stack she heard a cheery "Hello the house!"

When she dug herself out of the straw far enough to see, she knew it was her new friends, the Moore girls. They had long black curls, and were riding, of all things, a huge ox!

Phoebe hastily slid down the stack as Mother came from her hoeing and welcomed the visitors.

"But girls," Mother protested, "oxen can't be ridden! They are just to drive!"

The girls laughed and slid down the slick, dun-colored side of the animal, which was standing silently chewing.

"To be sure-r-r," one of them said, "people back along the way told us the same. But the teammate broke a leg in a prairie-dog hole and had to be shot, and Father-r couldn't drive just one, so when he bought another team, thr-r-ree or four-r of us rode this one before we knew — and then we were so in the habit we kept on riding."

They laughed merrily, and the girl who said her name was Maureen added, " 'Tis the advantage of being ignorant, you see."

She and her sister Kathleen joined in hunting for the hen. When it had finally been located in a clump of deep grass, and moved with the eggs to a coop, the Moore girls and Phoebe joined the younger children in sliding down the straw stack. They slid until they were all dusty and breathless, and then the girls gave David and Robbie a ride around the yard on their docile ox. Then they said they must start home, but urged Phoebe to come visit them soon, and Phoebe wrapped a pat of fresh butter and some Dutch cheese to send with them.

"What good times we're going to have with them!"

Phoebe exclaimed as she and Tessie watched the laughing girls, balanced on the broad back of the ox, start across the prairie.

Tessie echoed Hartley's verdict, "They're the most fun, Phoebe, all of them. It's grand to have neighbors, isn't it?"

But until the day of the house-raising, they had not realized how many neighbors they did have. Fourteen men, nine of them bringing families, had arrived by nine in the morning. Some came in wagons, two families came in surreys, several men and the whole Pfitzer family walked, and one couple came on horseback, with a baby in a papoose cradleboard fastened on the back of each. One of the babies was just learning to walk, and the other was less than two weeks old. The parents were only eighteen, and had taken up a claim four miles west, they said.

The women and the little children gathered in the house, where the newest baby was given the cradle, and the toddlers hid in their mothers' skirts seeking safety from so many strangers. The new women introduced themselves and the older settlers, like Mrs. Dawson and Mrs. Martin, said again and again how good it was to see the country building up.

The men and older boys went at once to the house site. The men knowingly felt the pieces of lumber — the walnut posts, the pine siding and floor boards. Mr. Martin and Mr. McNulty had built their own frame houses already, so they both considered themselves authorities. They disagreed on how to begin, and as each had a hot temper, a fight threatened before the day got well started. Mr. Dawson was trying vainly to calm them when the new neighbor, Mr. Pfitzer, said:

"Excuse, please, gentlemen, if I may be so good as to interrupt, in mine own country I am carpenter, making house all mine life; if is not some other gentlemans here is carpenters, I will be most glad to lay out the woods. In mine pack is tools."

He opened the leather pack which he had carried over on his back, disclosing a set of fine tools, with three saws, four hammers of various sizes and shapes, some planes and chisels, and much besides. That settled it.

Most of the men had never seen such fine tools, and Mr. Martin and Mr. McNulty alike began examining and admiring eagerly, while Mr. Sartin, the blacksmith, boomed, "Well, what do you know, Dutchy is a gen-u-ine carpenter. All right, Dutchy, where do we start?"

The boys were terribly disappointed that there would be no fight. They drifted off by themselves to play mumblety-peg with a jackknife in the dirt, while the men began doing dull things like measuring and figuring.

The Moore girls were sighted crossing the prairie on their ox, and the older girls walked to meet them. The animal stopped to graze on a choice patch of buffalo grass. The laughter of the girls rang across the distance, causing considerable distraction among the builders. All the men were interested in knowing how old the girls were, and then began teasing the single ones about who would have a chance to get a wife. Presently a wagon drove out of the

Moore dooryard bringing the rest of the family, and as they caught up with the reluctant ox, Mr. Moore snapped his whip like a pistol shot. The ox started off at a fast pace that nearly upset his riders, and passed the approaching escort. The girls had to turn and walk back, to meet the Moore girls in the Dawson yard after all.

Phoebe and some of the other girls carried buckets of hot coffee and fresh-fried doughnuts out to the men, who took turns drinking from the three big mugs available. The women meanwhile unpacked the baskets they had brought, and each drank from one of her own cups. Some of them dipped a doughnut in coffee and coaxed a shy child to show his face enough to take a bite. Presently some of the children forgot their strangeness with the temptation of food, and sat on the floor to munch their doughnuts. They stared at the other children as a preliminary to getting acquainted.

The weather was turning hot, although it was early in May. The women decided that by noon the shade of the house would be welcome, so they set up barrels on the north side, and on the barrels laid planks from the house lumber to make a long table. Each of the women had brought a cloth. Mrs. Moore's was a heavy, cream-colored, hand-woven linen. Next to it was Mrs. Pfitzer's, a neatly darned red-and-white-checked cotton. All along the table were laid the cloths to overlap, and then the plates or pans to eat from, and at one end the knives and forks and spoons were placed in neat piles.

As noon approached, the children were stationed around

the table with leafy switches to brush away the flies and the food was set out. Besides the many varieties of corn and corn-meal dishes, there were bowls of Dutch cheese, deviled eggs and creamed hard-boiled eggs, wild greens wilted in bacon grease and hot vinegar, dried beef with hominy, sauerkraut, raw cabbage slaw, and many kinds of potato salad.

There were kettles of stewed chicken, cold roast pheasant and partridge, fried rabbit, and Mrs. Pfitzer's rabbit stew with dumplings which she had carried across the fields in a big iron kettle. There was a kettle of boiled ham and beans, and a big baked ham. The special treat of the Dawsons was roast lamb with fresh mint sauce from Mother's mint bed. There was wheat bread, and soda biscuits, real treats for everyone, and of course the butter Phoebe had churned the day before, and many kinds of jelly and preserves. Last of all were the pies, dried apple and dried plum and dried peach; and gingerbread with a big bowl of whipped cream to spread on it, and Indian pudding, and thin, sweet pancakes spread with jam and rolled up while they were hot.

When the men were called, they went to the windmill tank to wash, then filed past the food, filling their plates with as much as they could heap on. Then they found places on the ground to squat while they ate and talked. The boys and little children ate next, and then the women and girls. Many returned again and again, slowing down toward the last but ready to get a taste of some special thing they had missed. Finally the last hungry boy admitted that, although he could still chew, he could no longer swallow.

While everyone was sitting around, Mr. Martin suddenly asked, "Dawson, what's this I hear about Indians coming while you were gone?"

And then Phoebe and Hartley and the little Dawsons found themselves the center of attention as their father proudly told of how the children had had to be left alone, and had cared for the sick Indian baby, and how Hartley had ridden the golden horse. The other children were admiring and envious.

The Moore girl, Kathleen, said, "Sure, that's the kind of neighbors to have close in an emergency; I can see you picked a good spot, Father."

"Aw," Gopher Martin, who was Hartley's age, sneered, "anyone could have done as much, I guess. I don't see so all-fired much about letting a squaw and papoose in out of the storm, and riding some old horse across the prairie a piece."

But Mr. McNulty said firmly, "It showed a deal of courage in them all. You've a family to be proud of, Dawson," and there was a general chorus of assent. Phoebe was very proud, and quite embarrassed to be the center of so much attention. But Hartley said, sounding much like his father:

"Oh, I don't know. As Gopher says, anyone would have done it."

And Phoebe was even prouder. She was glad Gopher Martin was not her brother.

After a brief rest, the men went back to sawing and pounding, while the women lingered over their coffee, exchanging recipes and taking little tastes of dishes they had not tried. For many it was the first pause since four or five in the morning.

By sundown, rafters outlined the new house, and the men were all pleased with their accomplishments. The women set out the leftover food and they all ate again, but this time there was no lingering. Mothers were packing baskets even while their husbands ate; the big boys had been fed first this time and then sent to harness the teams. Little children were hustled into the wagon beds. There was a general commotion of brothers and sisters quarreling over favorite places, and yelling good-bys at old and new friends, and mothers calling to laggards to get a hustle on, and boys shouting importantly at the teams with "Gee up" and "Whoa" and "Back! Back! You, Babe, Doc, back!"

"Thank you all — thank you," Father and Mother Dawson kept calling as one outfit after another rumbled out of the doorway and struck out across the prairie.

"Come around," they all shouted back.

Maureen and Kathleen Moore stayed to help wash the extra dishes and to talk over the day's events.

As they heard a song ringing out from the Martins' wagon, and then echoed from others, Kathleen asked, "Do you know the words of that? We heard it while we were coming out, but we never could catch it all."

For answer the Dawsons began singing:

"I am looking rather seedy now while holding down my
claim,
And my vittles are not always served the best,
And I hear the hungry coyote as he sneaks up through the
grass
To my little old sod shanty on the plain.
Oh, the hinges are of leather and the windows have no
glass,
And the sod roof lets the howling blizzard in,
But I would not trade with any man his life of ease and
gain
For my little old sod shanty on the plain."

There was a moment of silence, broken only by the faint,
faraway sounds of the departing neighbors.

Sadly Phoebe said, "Soon, now, we can't really sing it
any more."

The Moore girls laughed, and Maureen said, "You can
come to our place and sing it for a long time, I'm thinking.
And sure it's a grand song. Mother will dearly love it. Do
it again so we can get it good."

And so they began again, as Father and Hartley and
Tessie and the little boys went to the barn to milk, and to
the feed lot to gather cobs, and feed the pigs and shut up
the sheep. The Moore girls and Phoebe sang it as they
washed dishes at the outdoor table in the twilight. They
were still singing it when Mother took the little girls in to
get ready for bed.

Once the frames were up, the building seemed to go very fast. Mr. Moore and Mr. Pfitzer came often to help, and all the Dawsons worked at it, some helping and some hindering, according to their ages, but all wanting to be in on it. Mother and Phoebe held clapboards while the men nailed, and David and Robbie seemed always to have gone off with the hammer or the particular board that someone wanted. Martha carefully mixed several scoops of dirt into a batch of mortar that Hartley was stirring for the chimney bricks, and Mary Ann was in frequent danger of breaking her neck as she climbed at every opportunity up the ladders and along the open braces. But in spite of all of them, by late June, when the wheat was beginning to mellow from rich green to a tawny gold, the house was ready to move into.

It was almost square, with two stories. A big room went clear across the front downstairs, with the space behind it divided into a kitchen and a dining room. Upstairs there would be four rooms, just for sleeping. The upper part and the stairs were not finished yet, as Father could work on them in the winter when he could not be outside. But he moved the big bed over into the front room, and for the present the children would sleep around on the floor. The fresh, shiny yellow pine smelled good, but it seemed strange to have so much space.

Father hired Mr. Moore to haul some more supplies, extra nails they needed, the glass for the windows, and some wire screen to keep out the flies. And there was to be a new stove. It was a joyous day when he drove into the yard with the load.

Many of the settlers had little stoves in their soddies, and Mother had expected to buy a used one from a family that was giving up and going back. But Father said that after cooking in a fireplace that long, she deserved a new stove — and here it was.

The men and boys had a hard job lifting it down onto the ground, it was so heavy. Mother pranced around them impatiently, eager to get the wrappings off and see it. Everyone was quiet as she cut the ropes and pulled away the protective paper, and then a long "Oh" of admiration was followed by shouts and squeals.

It was a beautiful, shiny black, just the right height to stand at comfortably as it sat on its squat, curved black legs. Mother patted the top fondly, and Robbie pushed in to open the front door and disclose an oven which he promptly tried to crawl into. Hartley was already pushing the side draft doors, and calling, "Look, you can put wood or cobs in here without taking the pans off the top." Father pulled up a flat iron door on a hinge, on the right side, to show a deep tank where water could be heated.

While Mother was dusting it lovingly with the skirt of her petticoat, and exclaiming again and again, "Oh, Francis, it's beautiful! Just beautiful!" Father beamed and handed a big package to Phoebe.

"Here, daughter, see how these fit."

In the box Phoebe found shiny tin pans to fit the oven —

pans for pies and cakes, and a huge, deep one for raised bread.

"Oh, Mother, see! And now I can learn to really bake, can't I?"

"Me, too," said Tessie, and the little boys and Martha chimed in, "Me, too."

"Boys can't bake, can they, Mother?" Tessie objected.

"Of course they can," Father said. "Hartley and I and David and Robbie, we'll all bake, every man jack of us."

And Mother laughed and cried all at once, and then said to hide her feelings, "Well, now, this isn't getting the work done. We can't any of us bake until the stove is set up. Come, children, we'll get out of the road while the men finish."

The next day they carried the table and benches to the new house, and supplies of food. They would still use the soddy for storage until the upstairs was finished, and of course the dugout cave would still be the permanent place for storing food.

Even so, the soddy seemed strangely empty and forlorn as Phoebe went in for butter and cream for dinner; Mother and the little ones were in the new house, excitedly watching the first meal bubbling on the new stove, and each wanting a turn at poking in fuel. But for the first time in her memory, Phoebe was looking at the old fireplace cold at dinnertime, and it seemed sad and lonely. Where there had always been a table surrounded by hungry children, now there was only empty space, with the telltale marks of grimy hands on the whitewashed walls.

She thought of the many happy evenings with the family cozy before the fire, singing or telling stories; of the worry when the children were sick, or when the supplies of corn meal got low before the new crop was ripe. She thought of all the things she had done for the first time, which now seemed so easy and routine. And this was where she had stayed with the children through the big storm, with Mother and Father gone. That was when she had grown up, she thought. This was the place of her childhood, and it would never be the same again. Life in the new house would be exciting and fun, but it would never be like life in the soddy.

"Phoebe! Phoe-be!" Mother called impatiently. Quickly she grabbed the supplies and hurried out, feeling that she was leaving her childhood behind her.

CHAPTER 8

THERE WAS A GOOD WHEAT CROP THAT YEAR, WHICH ripened safely, and was cut and bound into sheaves. The rains came right for the corn, too, and it grew tall and thick. So did the everlasting sunflowers. All the children spent long days hoeing and hoeing.

The heat of July and August was unbearable, as always, but as always they bore it. This year they could eat with windows open and no flies, thanks to the wonderful new screens. There were, indeed, advantages to the new house, although it was so light, after the dimness of the soddy, that they all found it hard to sleep at first, and the thin wooden walls let the heat in much worse than the thick dirt walls had. Cooking on the new stove was wonderful fun.

In August came threshing, when the big steam outfit pulled into the barnyard and was set. Then the neighbors gathered again, the men and boys to thresh the wheat, and the women and children to cook and visit and play. Five new families had arrived during the summer. The country was building up fast.

Phoebe was to bake a big chocolate cake for the dinner.

Although she had made several that were quite good, she was anxious that such an important one should be successful. The evening before, she and Mother fed the family as early as possible, and then Mother set bread while Phoebe carefully creamed butter and sugar, and broke in eggs one at a time. Then she beat until she thought her arms would come off to be sure that she beat in enough air to make the cake light and fluffy. She wanted it to be all her own doing, but when Hartley offered to beat a while, she was glad to let him.

She had just set the oven dampers carefully, after Mother tested the heat with her hand and pronounced it right. She had chased the children out of the kitchen so that they would not jar the floor and make the cake fall (no danger of shaking the floor in the soddy, the children protested indignantly) when there was a sound of horses and a rumbling wagon, and shouts from the yard. Phoebe ran out to investigate.

"Phoebe! Hello! Hello, everyone!"

It was Marietta Stephens, driving the team herself, and in the wagon were her mother and all the little children. Father and Mother greeted them, and Father climbed up to help hand out children. Mrs. Stephens gave the baby to Mother while she climbed down. Then Hartley hopped up to drive the team to the barn and unharness it.

Father had seen one of the big boys at another neighbor's and sent an invitation for the family to come, but had not mentioned it to Phoebe for fear of disappointing her. But now here they were.

In the excitement of reunion, inspecting and admiring the baby, and getting the children acquainted with one another, and planning how the older children would sleep in the soddy to make room for Mrs. Stephens and the babies in the new house, Phoebe forgot her cake until Tessie said, "I smell something burning."

Then such a rushing, and consternation, and wailing! But it was only singed a little around the edges, as Hartley said. Mother trimmed off the scorched part and let the children eat it. Marietta and Phoebe visited and made thick chocolate frosting, and the cake was finally a success after all.

Tessie was delighted to have a baby to hold again, for Mary Ann was too lively now to sit on anyone's lap long. Phoebe and Mother wanted to hold the baby, too. Mother cooed over him, calling him "Marion" and insisting that he recognized his name. Tessie wanted him back, and Phoebe said, "I haven't held him at all, yet."

"He's my own, special baby," Mother said, "and how he has grown since I left him."

"He's my baby, too, Mother — remember, I helped take care of him for a month."

"Well," said Tessie, "he's mine, too — he's all of ours, because we stayed by our ownselves so you could go help him get born."

At that the pretty Mrs. Stephens kissed Tessie, and said, "You surely did, honey, and I think he'll always be part Dawson. I just hope he grows up to be such a fine, brave child as you all are."

There were new children who came with their families to the threshing, and again the Dawsons were asked to tell about their adventure with the Indian woman and baby and Hartley's ride on the wonderful Golden Chief. Hartley felt it almost made up for the fact that some of the boys and girls had come on their own ponies. Some of the horses were pretty good, but they were as nothing to the golden palomino.

The Stephenses stayed for five days, and after the hard work of threshing, the Dawsons and the Moores and the Pfitzers and the Stephenses took their dinners to the banks of the West Branch creek one day for a picnic. They found a tree strong enough to hold a swing, and the men put up a rope for the children. The women baked potatoes and roasting ears in a campfire, and they had brought fried chicken and apple pie. It was a wonderful outing, even though the creek had dried to little more than a muddy swamp, and the children made mud pies and set them to bake in an oven made of sticks.

When the Stephenses had left, Mother and Phoebe began drying corn and making pickles and sauerkraut. They dried apples, put sand plums into big jars of spring water to preserve them, shelled beans, and dried chunks of pumpkin on strings.

Days began early and ended late, and Tessie was given most of the care of the little girls. Father and Hartley were busy shocking corn, caring for the livestock, and trying to get more of the house finished before cold weather. The little boys worked in the garden and helped with the routine chores of carrying water and fuel. Everyone worked hard, rushing against time. Late summer was always a busy season, but this year there was the extra work of the house building. In addition, Father was anxious that as much as possible be accomplished before fall, because this winter there would be less help at home. Phoebe and Hartley and Tessie were to start to school.

Mother and Father had taught Phoebe and Hartley to read and cipher and write, and Tessie knew her letters and could count. But Father had started working for a school as soon as he came out, and now a schoolhouse had been built, three miles south on the prairie. A young man was coming from back east to teach it. Marietta Stephens and two brothers and a sister would come from on farther south, and other children from other directions. Mr. Dawson thought there might be twenty or twenty-five children in all.

Surely it would be fun, in some ways, and Hartley could hardly wait. But Phoebe felt a little sad whenever she thought of being away from her mother, and especially from the little ones, so much of the day. She didn't like things to change. She wished, often, that she could just turn back and live last year over again.

But the days went on, just the same. The nights grew cooler, and Father now was working all he could find time for to get the second floor into the house and the rest of the beds ready. Martha would have a little bed in her mother's and father's room to start with, and Tessie and Phoebe a big wide bed of their own. There would be two big beds in the boys' room; the little boys would sleep in one, and Hartley would have the other by himself except when some traveler or hired man needed to be put up for the night. Soon, Father said, he would build another bed in the girls' room, and Martha would move in with Tessie, and let Mary Ann have the trundle bed. Then Phoebe would have a big bed to herself, and could have Marietta come stay with her a while.

"But Mary Ann has plenty of room in the cradle, Father — she could sleep in it all winter."

"She would have enough room in the cradle by herself," Father grinned at Phoebe, "but I think she will be a little crowded if she has to share it."

"To share it? But who — oh, Father, do you mean we're going to have a new baby?"

Father went on pounding nails into the board Phoebe was holding for him, but he looked at her again and grinned. "You know, I wouldn't be the least bit surprised."

And then he was surprised, because Phoebe burst out crying. He dropped the hammer and picked her up as though she were still a little baby herself.

"Why, daughter, don't you like it? I thought you enjoyed the little ones. You've always been so good to help, maybe we have put too much on you. But things will be easier now; we'll try to see that you have more time to play. This has been a hard working year for all of us, but now the children will have room to play indoors in bad weather, and they can even play in the new barn; and cooking is easier with the new stove. You'll see, it will be all right."

Phoebe threw her arms around his neck and cried as he talked to her and patted her head. But as soon as she could make her voice work, she said:

"No, Father, it isn't that, at all. It's just — this one won't be my baby, because I'll be away at school all the time, and it will hardly know me. I just want to stay home with Mother and all of them. Hartley can go to school. He wants to. But I just want to go on like we have been."

Father laughed then, and kissed her wet cheeks. "So that's it! Well, you'll feel better, once you get into it."

"No, I won't! You don't know how I feel."

Father said, then, seriously, "Why don't I, Phoebe? And your mother, too. You hate to leave what you are used to, and you dread what you don't know. Everyone feels that way a little. How do you suppose your mother felt, leaving her family and friends, and the nice things she was used to back east, and coming all these miles and miles and miles out here beyond the railroads and beyond real roads, with two babies and no near neighbors? It was not easy, but it seemed the best chance for the family, and we came. Now I think she is very glad; I know I am. For our children are growing up healthy and independent, and with a good chance for the future.

"But women, as well as men, must train their minds, Phoebe. You have already seen, last winter, that you never know when you will need to be able to think fast and straight. And that is what school is for. That is why I have worked so hard to get a school started in our district. And when you have finished all that you can learn here, you're going to the state university; for the leaders of this state have already realized that a woman needs to be able to use her mind; they admit women with men to the same classes, and give them the same degree. One of these days, Phoebe Dawson, you are going to be a college graduate — but you have to start by going to school this fall."

Phoebe sat in his lap, rather dazed by his long speech, and all the ideas it opened out.

"But, Father, then what will I be? Why should I go to college? I don't think I want to be a teacher."

"Why, daughter, you will be, without doubt, the most important kind of teacher. Maybe you will decide that you would like to teach school for a while, but I am sure that eventually you will marry some fine young man, and teach your own children."

"But there will be schools by then everywhere."

"Oh, I don't mean just teach them to read and write. I mean something much more important. You must teach them how to live. And you must help this state grow into a good state to live in, a state that takes care of its people as a family takes care of its children. I don't know just how; but that is why I want you children to have the best education you can get, so you can find out how. I don't suppose it will be easy. But I am sure you will do it."

He smiled at her so confidently, Phoebe could only smile back and promise, "Yes, Father."

CHAPTER 9

ONE AFTERNOON SHORTLY AFTER PHOEBE'S TALK WITH HER father, she and Tessie and their mother were sewing by the pleasant south window of the new house. Mother and Phoebe were making school dresses, a blue one for Phoebe, a green one for Tessie. Tessie was making little dresses from the scraps for her doll and Martha's. Mother sang to the children and rocked Mary Ann's cradle with her foot. But Phoebe was thinking her own thoughts, dreaming of school, and wondering if she might like it after all, with a new blue dress and her blue necklace. Just two more weeks!

Suddenly Hartley burst into the room. "Where's Father?" he demanded, excitedly.

"I don't know, dear — outside, somewhere. What's wrong?"

"One of the Martin kids just rode over. His mother sent him, but made him promise to hurry right back, for their father is away. There have been Indian raids on beyond them, and a huge band of Indians has been sighted coming this way. Pete Martin was on their field windmill and saw them. He said there were thousands! They weren't due to hit his folks' place unless they changed their course, but he says his mother's fit to be tied."

Mrs. Dawson picked up Mary Ann. "Phoebe," she said, quietly, "get all the children into the soddy. Hartley, find your father if you can. He surely is not far. If you don't find him at once, put the stock into the old sod barn. They may burn the frame buildings, if they are drunk or mad about something. But they probably are just trying to get stock. Quick, now. We will be safe in the soddy."

They were already on their way as she finished, and in a matter of moments the new house was empty. As soon as the children were settled, Phoebe ran out to help Hartley. Then they looked all around the place once more for their father.

Hartley went up the windmill for a quick look. He stared a moment toward the west. Then he almost slid back down the ladder. His face was white and scared.

"Run for the house, Phoebe," he shouted. "They're coming! And they've got Father!"

Phoebe ran, with Hartley catching up with her as they reached the soddy. Their mother was tense, but calm. When they had told her, she stood silent a moment.

"What shall we do, Mother? What shall we do?"

"You're sure it was Father?"

"Yes, I know it was. He was on Captain. I remembered, when I saw Captain gone from the corral, Father said he was going over to see how the water in the creek was holding up. And he and a tall Indian on a pinto were together, and behind them were ever and ever so many. Mother, what shall we do?"

"Nothing, I think," she said slowly. "If they mean harm, anything we would try would make it worse for Father. But I think he is safe. There has been no real Indian violence around here since before we came out. The Indians feel we have stolen their land, and some of them try to get back by taking our stock. I expect they will do that, and then let Father go."

"Oh, Mother! The new work horses, and everything? Whatever will we do?" Phoebe wailed.

"The Lord has kept us, Phoebe. We must trust him, and do our best. Perhaps we have no right to the land. I've never quite felt the Indians got a square deal. Anyway, crying won't help.

"Go to the door and tell me as soon as you see them. Hartley, were they coming fast?"

"No, at a slow walk, right across the fork of the creek."

"Then run bring us more water, and keep a sharp lookout."

Hartley did as he was told, understanding his mother's thoughts. With plenty of water, and all the food stored in the soddy, the family could stay inside and out of the trouble for quite a while, if the Indians did not really come to harm them. He ran out, and as best he could ran back with the full bucket. As he emptied the bucket into the water barrel, Phoebe cried out: "There they are! Father and . . ."

At that moment a great shout went up outdoors, Mrs.

Dawson slammed the door shut, and Hartley dropped the bucket. He put his arm around his mother. The shouting increased, and there seemed all at once to be crowds of stamping horses and yelling people all around them. Then the noise died down somewhat, and the listeners heard their father's deep, ringing voice.

"Hart — ley! Phoe — be! Where are you?"

They looked at their mother, and she looked at them.

"Shall we go?" Phoebe asked.

Hartley moved bravely toward the door, but not very quickly. Before he could open it he heard his father's voice again, just outside. "I'll look in here, maybe they are all in here doing something, just a minute . . ." and the door opened. There he was, grinning at them like Christmas.

"Well, Hartley, Phoebe, are you suddenly deaf?" he asked a little impatiently, but laughing. Then he caught sight of his wife's face.

"Why, Marian — what's wrong?"

"Francis — aren't you — are they — we thought you were captured! Martins sent word there had been raids . . ." She stumbled over the words, trying to understand the new situation. The younger children came crowding to their father, and as he understood their mistake he threw back his head and laughed and laughed.

Then he kissed his wife, and said: "Marian, you're the bravest girl in the county, only there is no danger. Come, we have guests. Run on out, children," he said to Hartley and Phoebe. "I think you will find some old friends — and a great many new ones." He swung Martha to his shoulder and put his arm around his wife, who was still bewildered.

"Come on, come on, everyone," he commanded, and went out into the sunshine with the little ones scampering after.

Outside, Phoebe and Hartley had discovered old friends indeed. Chief Flying Hawk on his palomino, his daughter-in-law on the beautiful Golden Chief, with the papoose's black eyes staring from over her shoulder, and beside her a tall, handsome young man on a graceful pinto. He was the one Hartley had seen his father riding with, and now he guessed that it was Flying Hawk's son, the father of the baby. Ranged around the yard were many other Indians, men and young boys, and behind them women, girls and little children, all on beautiful horses.

They all seemed in very good spirits, yelling among themselves and milling around. Hartley and Phoebe, however, felt shy with so many people looking at them. Hartley raised his hand timidly and smiled a little at Flying Hawk, and then ventured to step closer and stroke the nose of his friend, Golden Chief. The big golden horse nickered and rubbed against Hartley. At this, for some reason, a great shout went up again from the visitors, and some of the young men reared their own horses to show their feelings.

Phoebe had stepped over to greet the baby and its mother, but now at the new shout she suddenly stopped and looked back at her father. He stood, with her mother, close outside the door, the excited little ones clinging to them. He laughed and waved Phoebe on.

"You are not very hospitable, daughter," he said. "Go welcome your guests."

The Indians seemed to be waiting. Chief Flying Hawk's stern face softened when she told him "welcome," and he nodded at her. Phoebe shyly said to the young mother, "Baby not sick?"

The mother spoke rapidly to the young man beside her, who nodded in seeming approval. Then he spoke to her, and swung down off his horse. He lifted the baby out of the sling where it was riding on its mother's back, and set it on its feet on the ground. The little one delightedly took several wobbly steps, then toppled over to be caught in its father's arms. Phoebe laughed and clapped her hands, and Hartley did, too.

Chief Flying Hawk then said, "The son of my son becomes strong and walks. The people of Flying Hawk have not forgotten that friends saved him from the big storm and from sickness."

Another great shout from the assembled Indians, while the baby's father, standing now between Phoebe and Hartley, nodded again and the young mother smiled softly at them.

The chief went on with his speech. "Flying Hawk has welcomed the friends of his son's son as members of the tribe."

Another shout.

"All of the tribe of Flying Hawk are famous riders. By campfires all across the prairie, people tell of the beautiful horses of Flying Hawk's people, and of the skill of the young men who ride them."

A loud shout!

"The new friend has shown he is a worthy horseman, for he has ridden the great Golden Chief, which no other man has ever done."

Another shout, and Hartley stood very straight. So much attention focused on them, Phoebe could hardly breathe. The chief now paused, backed his horse slightly, and at the same time, the young mother, with just a brush of her moccasin on the flank of Golden Chief, backed and partially turned him. The other Indians began moving forward until they quickly were drawn up in two lines facing each other, making a long empty aisle about the width of a roadway, with Phoebe, Hartley and the chief's son, holding the baby, at the end of it.

What were they doing? Phoebe's and Hartley's eyes met. They were equally puzzled. Chief Flying Hawk began to speak.

"It is to the honor of the people of Flying Hawk that every young man of the tribe shall have a worthy horse when he is ready for it. And she who has nursed the son of the chief's son should likewise have a worthy horse. Therefore, the son of the son of Flying Hawk is honored to present to his friends — these two new friends."

Here, Flying Hawk raised his right arm high, a terrific shout exploded throughout the ranks of the visitors, and there came whirling around the far end and down the empty space between the two lines of Indians, four abreast — two

"You mean they are ours?" gasped Hartley

young Indian men on black and white pintos, leading between them — two beautiful matched golden horses. They
raced straight toward the group at the end of the aisle.
Phoebe wanted to run, but the chief's son, holding his
child, never moved a muscle and Hartley stood straight
beside him. So Phoebe braced her toes and prayed that
those thundering feet would stop before they trampled her.

Only a few feet away all four horses suddenly stopped
in their tracks. The cheers broke out again, as the chief's
son held his baby's hand to reach for the bridle of the
golden stallion and put it into the hand of Hartley, and
then for the bridle of the mare, and put it into Phoebe's
hand. Both children were so stunned they had hardly
strength to hold the leather straps, but the horses moved
and stood quietly.

Mr. Dawson said, from just behind them, "Well, Phoebe,
Hartley, can't you thank the Chief — and his grandson?"

"Father, you mean they're ours?" gasped Hartley.

"To keep?" asked Phoebe.

"That's what I understand," Father said, looking at the
Indian chief and laughing. Phoebe and Hartley looked at
each other, and then at the gorgeous creatures, standing so
quietly at the ends of their lines.

All the Indians crowded closer and closer, watching the
children and seeming to enjoy their surprise. The horses
were beautifully matched in color, just a shade lighter than
Golden Chief, and only slightly smaller. They had his
silky creamy mane and tail, and the same high lift of the
head. Hartley's was a solid color, while Phoebe's had a

creamy star between its eyes and four creamy white stockings.

But as they stuttered and mumbled, trying to get words out to express their great delight, the young mother swung down from Golden Chief and came toward the children with some bright cloth over her arms. She handed to Phoebe a woven blanket, of brown and orange and yellow and cream, and to Hartley one of black and white with a little bright green.

As she smiled at them, Flying Hawk explained, "The wife of my son also wishes to show her friends that she has not forgotten their kindness."

Meanwhile the young woman walked past Phoebe and Hartley to give a third blanket, a solid cream with fine brown lines, to Tessie, who was shyly gripping her father's hand.

The chief went on, "When there will be a little colt," he nodded toward the mare at Phoebe's side, "it will go under the blanket of the small one. Together they will grow up, and when the legs of both are long, they, too, will ride the prairies."

The Indians all whooped again. The Indian mother smiled at Tessie, and said, "Girl good. Little girl," she held her hand low to Tessie's head, "work big," and held her hand high to her own head.

Mrs. Dawson understood and nodded. "Yes, she is still a little girl, but she helps like a woman."

"Yes. Little woman. Good."

Then she turned, sprang onto Golden Chief, took the

baby from her husband and fastened it into the sling on
her back. The Indians all began wheeling and backing their
horses. Chief Flying Hawk and his family rode through and
took the lead, and off they all rode once more into the west.

Hartley and Phoebe at last began to believe! They each
had a beautiful, golden palomino.

Hartley threw his arms around the neck of his, exclaiming, "Oh, you beauty. You're mine. My own horse, and I
never really thought I would have one. And such a horse!"

Phoebe more cautiously patted the nose of hers, admiring it out loud. "See, what a beautiful color. It just shines,
doesn't it, Mother? And the darling white star! I'm sorry
yours doesn't have a star and stockings, Hartley."

"Huh! I've been sorry yours wasn't all pure gold like
mine. Look how he stands!"

Robbie asked, "Can we ride them, too? Can we, Hartley?" and David chimed in, "Me, too. I want to ride, too."
They were just beginning to recover from their tremendous
awe of the Indians.

"Do you suppose they have been broken, Father?" Hartley asked, eager for a ride, but not quite sure.

"You will find they have been beautifully trained, I
think," their father said. "All spring and summer the chief's
son has been teaching them, just for you. He even tied a
blanket around his waist and rode yours, Phoebe, so she
would not be afraid of skirts."

"And we can ride them right now?"

"I think so. Chief Flying Hawk says they are quite safe
and gentle, for their friends. And I trust his judgment on a

horse, any day. Now then, Marian, what are you crying about?"

"I am not crying," his wife said, wiping her eyes. "But anyway, how do you know all about them?"

"Yes, Father, how do you know?"

Father now was patting the stallion, rubbing his back and flank and legs, and then he tossed Hartley's new blanket on. The horse quivered, but stood quite still.

"He seems perfectly gentle. Well, a few weeks ago I got to wondering again if I could possibly manage to get another horse. Even a stodgy, fairly old horse would do for a while, for you had all helped so much with the work, I was making out fairly well. And there will be a lot of weather not fit either for the buggy or sleigh, and Captain could not carry three of you. So unless we had another horse, some of you would miss a lot of school . . ."

"Yes, Francis," Mother interrupted, "I know you wanted to get them a horse, even if you couldn't afford it. Go on."

"Well, I heard Flying Hawk and his people were going to move this fall. They are going farther southwest, for more grazing for the horses and sheep. And I thought he might have some horse, still spirited but too old to be very valuable, that would serve our purposes, and that he might let me have cheap rather than take it along. So when I was down on the west branch a few weeks ago to look at the cattle there, I took a day to ride on over. They were camped not very far beyond.

"When I told him what I wanted, you should have heard him laugh. And then he let me in on their secret. The whole tribe was having a great time over it. They love to give, you know, and certainly these are gifts anyone can be proud to give."

"And you never told us!"

"And spoil all this show? Of course not! What do you take me for?"

"Well, Francis," his wife said, "I still don't see that you need scare me to death, letting me think you were in trouble."

"How was I to know you'd cook up a silly idea like that? And anyway," he added teasingly, "I didn't really figure anyone would mind if the Indians did go off with me."

This brought loud protests, of course, except from his wife, who said he just wanted to be bragged on. Meanwhile Hartley was leading his horse around the dooryard, talking to him, and Father was testing Phoebe's and putting the blanket on.

"What do you say, sister? Want to try her out?" he asked.

Phoebe did! Hartley had had two rides on Golden Chief, but she had never even once ridden a good horse. She would have liked to leap up as the Indian woman did, but it looked like a long way. So for a start she let Father lift her foot. She felt a little uncertain up on the strange broad back.

"She's higher than Captain," Phoebe observed, looking at the ground. Father and Mother both laughed.

"She is that," Mother said.

"Sit tight," said Father. So Phoebe held firm with her knees and walked the horse around the yard. When Hartley saw Phoebe was up, he jumped onto his, with no trouble except that the horse jumped sideways a few times. But Hartley got a firm seat, and challenged Phoebe to a race.

To his great disgust, Father said they must just walk quietly in the dooryard.

"I loped Golden Chief," Hartley protested.

"I know you did, but don't let it go to your head. Golden Chief is a seasoned horse, wise and dependable. These are two-year-olds, not sure yet themselves what they are going to do next. They are just like young kids. You are strange to them, and so is the place. They might get excited and take it into their heads to go home. If they did, the likes of you, or me either, would not turn them. They can be led but not forced, just as you saw with Golden Chief. And if they dashed off with you and showed up at the camp, wouldn't you feel foolish?"

Hartley realized that he would, and submitted to walk his horse around and around the house and barn.

"What are their names?" Phoebe asked.

"You can choose your own," Father said.

"Then I'm going to name mine Star. Twinkling Star, in fact, because she goes in a twinkling."

Hartley said, "I'm going to name mine Pal — because he's a Pal-o-Mine. Get it?"

"We get it, son," Father said, laughing, "and I suppose if you like it, it is as good a name as any for a palomino."

Only the deepening twilight finally persuaded Phoebe and Hartley to put Pal and Star to bed in the new barn. Even then they wanted to take their own blankets and sleep in the stable, and several times during the evening they were sure that they heard sounds like horse thieves.

"In the morning," they promised the others, "we will take you all riding. Every single one."

"Can I ride, too?" asked Tessie.

"Of course, for you must begin to get ready for your own little colt. You have been wanting a baby, Tessie. That will truly be your own baby," Father told her.

"Us, too? Robbie and me, too?" David demanded.

"Yes, indeed, my men. In other years, when Pal and Star have some more babies, they will be for you."

"Do you mean," Robbie asked, "they are going to have thousands and thousands of baby horses?"

"Well, not that many. But I trust we are not going to have thousands and thousands of children, either, although sometimes in the soddy it did seem as though there were that many. But they will have some colts, if all goes well, and there is a pretty good chance you can each have a horse by the time you are Hartley's and Phoebe's ages.

"You see," he went on, "Chief Flying Hawk not only has given you two very valuable horses, but by giving you a pair like that, he has given you a chance to build up a fine herd of your own, if you take very good care of them. You can trade some of them, after a while, to get new breeding stock, and by the time you are ready for college, you should have resources of your own to pay your whole board and room while you are away."

"Could I take Pal to college?" asked Hartley. "Because if I can't, I don't want to go."

Father laughed. "Well, I never heard of a horse at the university, but we never know what might happen by then. But I'll tell you where Pal can go, in just two weeks."

"I know," Hartley shouted. "To school."

"That's right. To the opening day at District 13 School. Pal and Star and Captain, for Tessie, you must have Captain now for your own horse until your new colt comes and grows up. And the rest of us will just have to beg rides from all of you."

"Can I use my new blanket on Captain?" Tessie asked.

"To be sure. I expect he will be so proud he will even try to run away." This was such a funny idea they all laughed.

Then Hartley said, "Oh, Phoebe, won't it be just perfectly splendid to come tearing into the schoolyard and stop bing! just like that — like the Indians did this afternoon! Just think, Phoebe, of going to school on Pal and Star. I'm going sort of late the very first day, so I can swoop in and surprise them all."

Phoebe smiled. She had no intentions of any such wild entrance as Hartley planned. She would arrange her blue dress neatly, so that it would not be mussed. She would have the blue necklace exactly in place between the ruffles, and blue pieces tied on the ends of her braids. Her lunch and books would be in a neat package, and she would sit very straight, and canter gracefully up to the door, and slide down casually, as though she were a fine lady and had been riding her own fine horse every day since she was born.

That night, as they lay on their blankets by the window nearest the stable, Hartley whispered, "Phoebe."

"Yes?"

"Don't you feel lots more than a year older than you did this time last year?"

"Yes. If anyone had asked me then if we could do all the things we have, I'd have said 'no' for sure. But we did them, staying alone, and everything."

"Yes," Hartley agreed. "I guess school will be the same way. It's sort of hard, thinking about it, but I guess when it comes, we can do it."

Phoebe had not realized that he, too, had qualms. It made her feel a little braver as she felt the need to encourage him.

"I guess, Hartley, it's really true, like Father says, 'nothing succeeds like trying.' "

And she discovered, as she lay thinking of the adventures of the past year and the uncertainty of the future, that she really believed it herself.